The Hidden Amethyst

J.C. Buchanan

to the incredible
Kelsey!

♡, J.C. Buchanan
"Purple"

DEDICATION

This book is lovingly dedicated to
Steve, Jeremiah, & Sawyer

CONTENTS

1   In the Asylum

2   Mr. Jeremiah Chuckchester

3   Amethyst's Punishments

4   All aboard the Orphan Train!

5   Blowing Misadventures

6   Meeting Mary

7   Asylum Quiana

8   Back on the Dismal Train

9   Queen Mahalia's Castle

10 Shrieking, a Plan, and a Little Mixed-up
    Wish

11 A Little Bit of Airplane Trouble

12 Castle Again?

13 Rome Street!

14 Lucy is Startled

15 Meet the Mochas

16 What's up with the Mochas?

17 Marissa the Rag Doll

18 A Very Peculiar Rubber Band

19 Dr. Sawyer

20 The Return of Avery Mocha

21   Attack!

22   Steve Mocha

23   The Plan

24   A Magic Ring

25   Back to Asylum Odelia

26   Rebecca, Kayla, Delaney and Miranda

27   McKenna and a Bowl

28   Boxcar Thoughts

29   Jump

30   Check-up on the Twins

31   Goodnight

32   Time to Get Moving

33   Two Reappearances

34   At Dr. Sawyer's

35   For All We Know

36   Miranda is Reunited with the Twins

37   Nora! Oh no!

38   Family Gathering

39   Back on Boxcar 24

40   "Marshibilsn!"

41.   Fairies!

      Epilogue\\

4.12.12

Chapter one
In the Asylum

The day started out badly.

First of all, Amethyst woke up late.

When she woke up she was faced with the headmistress's wrinkled old face, which was glaring at her.

Amethyst shrieked.

"Shut your mouth, you nasty girl," said Miss Odelia. "If you scream again you'll greatly regret it."

"What did I do wrong?" stammered Amethyst, even though she knew all too well what she had done.

"What do you think?" growled Miss Odelia. "You woke up late! It's an hour past wake-up time!"

Amethyst looked at the clock. It read 8:30. She stifled a groan.

"Get up," ordered Miss Odelia. "And yes- you're being punished. You cannot get dressed today. You must go around in pajamas. Oh, and no showers for a week."

Amethyst was horror-stricken, and not because she would be embarrassed. Her pajamas were as light as... well.... feathers! She'd freeze in a heartbeat! Especially on such a cold day! The place had no furnace. Well, it did, but the vents in the girls' rooms and the ones in the cafeteria were turned off, so girls slept, dressed, and ate in utter coldness in the winter, and utter hotness in the summer. (Which, in Amethyst's opinion, hotness was much better than coldness.)

At least the schoolrooms are warm, thought Amethyst. If I stay there most of the day I should be okay.

But still, she looked up to Miss Odelia with pleading and asked, "But ma'am, if you don't mind me saying so, I will freeze if I stay in this thin nightgown!"

"Exactly," retorted Miss Odelia with a triumphant grin. Then her smile faded as she realized what she had just said.

"Oops. Uh, what I mean is, uh, well...."

At that moment Amethyst's teacher, Mrs. Vancolia, came into the room. Miss Odelia quieted down in surprise and said, "Why, hello, Mrs. Vancolia."

"Same to you," barked Mrs. Vancolia. "I'm here to retrieve my student. Why is she in her bedgown, ma'am?"

"She.... is being punished," said Miss Odelia hesitantly.

"Well," said Mrs. Vancolia shortly, "do something different to her. I'm not having a girl in pj's embarrassing my class in front of all the others. Now get her dressed and bring her down."

Amethyst breathed a sigh of relief. Mrs. Vancolia was horrible, there was no mistaking that, but she did have a weakness that came in handy sometimes, and that weakness was she hated to be embarrassed.

Miss Odelia nodded at her. "But of course, Mrs. Vancolia."

"You thought that since that dumb teacher has a weakness you'd get the upper hand," she growled, "but you're wrong. Now up and out, and don't bother to snag breakfast, or lunch, or dinner, for Mahalia's sake." That was a phrase Miss Odelia enjoyed using.

So, thought Amethyst, no food today and no clothes. Pretty bad.

"By the way," said Miss Odelia, "tell that dumb teacher that the reason you are still wearing pj's is because pj's are the new style. I will be asking her during lunch if you said the right thing. If you didn't, you will be severely punished."

Amethyst nodded weakly. She asked for a drink of water, got it, and followed Miss Odelia out of the room.

When she got to her classroom, the warmness felt as good on her skin as a feast would feel on her empty stomach. She marched into the room proudly, gathering in the glorious, wonderful warmth.

Mrs. Vancolia eyed her carefully.

Amethyst remembered Miss Odelia's words and her excitement faded away. "Uh, um, pj's are the new style," she whispered faintly.

Mrs. Vancolia's eyes lit up. "They are? Oh yippee! I've just been dying for a new style!"

Amethyst nodded and took her seat. Some of her classmates looked at her funny. She returned the gaze, as if to say, You know very well this is not my fault.

She barely knew anybody.

At asylums like these it was hard to make friends because everybody felt so miserable all the time. She did have some friends, Miranda and Victoria, but she was not close to them, they only slept in the same room. Amethyst twisted around in her chair to see Miranda behind her. Her so-so friend gave her an encouraging smile. Victoria was three grades ahead of Amethyst so they were not in the same class.

Finally, class was over, but Amethyst wasn't as pleased as she normally was. The cafeteria, with her pajamas on, would be a nightmare! She raised her hand timidly as the rest of the class leaked into the cafeteria.

"Yes, Amethyst?" said Mrs. Vancolia absentmindedly.

She was writing furiously at her desk, her glasses tilted on her tiny, sharp nose. Her grayish hazel eyes moved back and forth across the paper, and her chubby fingers clutched the pencil like she was holding onto it for dear life. Her grayish hair drooped in front of her, coming out of its bun. Her hair was covered in bobby pins, as if she had tried- unsuccessfully- to keep her hair up.

She probably has trouble keeping hair on top of such a fat head, thought Amethyst. It was true. From her fat, round head to her chubby toes, the teacher was engulfed in fat.

"Uh," said Amethyst. "Could I, um, kinda, like, skip lunch, please?"

Mrs. Vancolia raised her eyebrows. "And why is that, Miss Amethyst? I'd think you'd want to show off your new style."

"Um, it's not that, Mrs. Vancolia," said Amethyst nervously. "It's just that.... well..." Suddenly her growling stomach gave her the excuse. "It's just that I'm not really hungry," she lied. It was totally false - in fact she was starving - but she did not want to be cold again.

"How can that be?" mused Mrs. Vancolia, stopping her work to admire her fingernails, which were painted a hideous orange, just like Miss Odelia's. "You skipped breakfast, and you just picked at your food last night."

"Miss Odelia said-" started Amethyst, but then reconsidered. Boy would she get into trouble if she was caught disobeying Miss Odelia's orders, but Mrs. Vancolia was right. She had skipped breakfast and barely ate her dinner the night before. She had had a good reason for it- it was sloppy, gross slop, like the stuff pigs eat, some type of stew filled with pieces of banana, bread crusts, and more Amethyst did not want to think about.

She focused back on the present. She could tell Mrs. Vancolia she actually did want to eat lunch, and risk getting into BIG trouble, and basically freeze, or she could try to survive in warmth on a growling, empty stomach.

Amethyst considered the ups and downs of both. If she didn't eat lunch, she risked not getting food for a few days, because most likely all the food would be slop. But if she risked eating, she'd get punished, but she'd get food, and not slop. She knew it was food for today's lunch because there had been a huge sign outside the cafeteria that read, "Today's lunch- not slop!"

"What did she say, Amy?" said Mrs. Vancolia, who now was admiring her toes, which were propped up on her desk.

"She said I could eat lunch," said Amethyst, "and my name is Amethyst."

"Amethyst is too fine a name for an orphan," said Mrs. Vancolia. Amethyst didn't bother reminding her she wasn't an orphan. "Anyway," said Mrs. Vancolia, "why did you want to stay if you have permission to eat and you have a new style to show off?"

"I guess you're right," lied Amethyst, making her decision. "I do want to show off. Thank you for reminding me I was wearing the new fashion."

Mrs. Vancolia fluttered her eyelashes. "Any day," she said. "I love fashion."

Amethyst nodded, and dashed off to lunch before Mrs. Vancolia could realize Amethyst had lied.

Staying out of Miss Odelia's sight, Amethyst got into the cafeteria line and let out a sigh of relief that it wasn't slop. It looked like cream of mushroom soup, with a white broth and little gray blobs. She also thought she spotted some noodles.

Amethyst helped herself to a large bowl of the soup, a tall glass of water, and a piece of bread slathered with butter. Then she sat down at a large table in hopes she wouldn't be noticed.

Nobody at the table noticed her. There were a few girls from her class, but the rest of them weren't. Nobody was talking, as usual. Everyone was eating silently, and not just at her table, but through the whole place. There were not many groups of friends at the asylum, but the few that were there were quietly chatting.

Amethyst took a sip of soup. The hot, creamy soup slid down her throat. Ah. The bread was buttery, the soup creamy, the water cold.

Amethyst had just finished her meal and was about to go back for seconds when she spotted Miss Odelia staring at her with fire blazing in her eyes.

What could she do? Amethyst panicked. Maybe she could casually walk away and sit down in her classroom, and Miss Odelia would think she was imagining things. She decided on it, and picked up her soup bowl and cup, casually walked across the room, dumped her dishes in the large sink, and exited the cafeteria.

But as she was exiting, she bumped into a body. The body yelped and Amethyst realized it was Mrs. Vancolia!

"Amy!" yelled Mrs. Vancolia. "You brat, you lied to me! Oooooodeeellaaa!" she called.

Miss Odelia was over in a second and had Amethyst's wrist in her hand. Mrs. Vancolia grabbed her other wrist.

"Let go!" cried Amethyst, struggling against her captors.

Miss Odelia and Mrs. Vancolia exchanged a glance, and then they picked Amethyst straight off the floor and carried her upstairs to her room, which she shared with seven more girls.

It was a tiny room; the eight teeny beds crammed together, barely as long as Amethyst; the pillows were leaking feathers and flat; the blankets provided barely any warmth, as they were practically threadbare and every girl only had one. On especially cold nights, the girls would sleep under the sheets covering the mattresses.

The room was painted an ugly yellow color with rubber duckies on the wallpaper. The fan was rusty but worked, and the girls would turn it on on hot summer nights, if they could get it on without Miss Odelia catching them. The light had four bulbs but only two worked.

Amethyst glanced at her own bed and cringed. The bed was unmade, the blanket crumpled in a ball on the bed. The sheet was stripped off the mattress and laying on top of the blanket. The mattress was leaking stuffing. Amethyst thought about using the mattress as a blanket, too.

Mrs. Vancolia and Miss Odelia tossed Amethyst on the bed, and instantly she grabbed the blankets and pulled them around her. It helped her cold body, but not much.

Miss Odelia gestured for Mrs. Vancolia to leave, and then turned to Amethyst. "Make all these beds. I want them to look professional. When you're done, get the washrags and mops and mop the floors, even under the beds. When you're done, remake the beds. Then clean the bathroom until it shines. Then I want you to get the wallpaper glue and glue the torn parts of the wallpaper back up." After Miss Odelia left, Amethyst fainted.

chapter two
Mr. Jeremiah Chuckchester

When Amethyst recovered from her faint, she got up woozily and thought about what she had to do. She could probably get away with only making the beds once. So she got the mop and began to scrub the floors.

It took her a half hour to finish. When she was done, her arms ached and her knees stung from soap that got into her cuts. Plus, she was hungry again. But at least moving around kept her warmer.

Next, she took off her shoes, found a towel, and dried the floor. While she did it, she wondered why Miss Odelia wanted all this done.

There must be an inspector coming, figured Amethyst. *I bet Miss Odelia is punishing lots more girls, too, and making them clean the cafeteria, their rooms, or the classrooms!*

Amethyst finished drying and began pushing the beds back

together. Then she reconsidered. Would the inspector like it if the beds were squished together? But then she realized there was no other way. So she shrugged, made the beds (which she thought was the funnest part) and plumped the pillows. She could've done it badly, so it didn't pass inspection, but she was too afraid of Miss Odelia's wrath. So she did it right.

Next she started on the disgusting wallpaper.

* * * * * * * * * * * * * * * * *

When Amethyst was finally done, her hands were grubby, sticky, dirty, wet, slimy, and numb. Her knees were bleeding and her hair was a mess. Her feet were covered in grime from the floor.

She sighed, and went into the tiny bathroom, where she washed her hands with lots of soap. Then she turned on the shower and rinsed her hair.

Just as she was finishing, Miss Odelia came into the room. "Beds made, floor clean, wallpaper glued.... drat. The girl's done everything. But where is the little brat?"

Amethyst jumped a little, rubbed her golden blonde hair with a towel, and went into the room. "I'm here, Miss Odelia."

"Okaaaay," said Miss Odelia, "why is your hair damp?" Amethyst's hand flew to her hair. Drat, it was still damp. "My hair was gross," she said. "So I'd thought I'd wash it. I didn't think you liked gross hair." Silently, she added, *I thought you would punish me if my hair was not clean.*

"I don't," said Miss Odelia, fighting back anger. "Now, is the bathroom clean?"

Amethyst thought. Had she washed it? Yes. "It's just a bit wet, ma'am," she said obediently.

"Let me see." Miss Odelia pushed past Amethyst and saw the sparkling bathroom. She let out a yelp.

"What is it?" asked Amethyst, trying not to get on Miss Odelia's nerves.

"You.... you... you did it correctly," stammered Miss Odelia. "Um, good job. Now, I want you to brush your hair, wash your face.... pamper yourself. In a bit Rachel and Emmy are coming up. Help them, too. When you're all done come downstairs and I'll give you your clothing."

So the inspector is coming, thought Amethyst and bit back a whoop and a groan. To make the asylum look good, every time the inspector came every girl was spoiled silly and the whole place was heated, not just the classrooms.

But she groaned because Rachel and Emmy were the most troublesome kids at the asylum. They were twins, both age four, and made a mess everywhere. Getting them ready would be a nightmare! But still, she didn't want to get into trouble, so she said, "Yes, ma'am."

"Oh, and Amy?" Clearly Miss Odelia thought Amethyst was too fine a name also. "Victoria is coming up later to get ready too. By that time you must be ready and Rachel and Emmy must be, too."

Oh dear, thought Amethyst. *It will take a lot more than an hour to get those two ready!* So she bit her lip and asked, "Is it okay if I ask for help?"

* * * * * * * * * * * * * * * * * *

A half hour later, Amethyst was deflated, along with Miranda, who had come to help out.

Both of them were lying on their beds face-down, while Emmy and Rachel were in the bathroom. Toothpaste was all over the sink. Water covered the tiles. Hair lay in bunches all over the bathroom, thanks to Emmy's attempt to brush Rachel's hair. The once-clean towels were now unrecognizable with mouthwash, makeup, and other toiletries. A brush was on the floor, and an opened lipstick was in the toilet, making the water an unappetizing pink. Makeup lay in gobs all over the already wet floor. And that was all because of the two monsters. Right now the two were coloring on each other with eye shadow and face cream, giggling all the while.

Speaking through the blanket, Miranda said, "Those two are little human monsters."

"You can say that again," groaned Amethyst. "I'm going to have to clean that whole bathroom again."

"It'll be hard," agreed Miranda, "but I'll help you." She shivered. "Is it any warmer in the bathroom?"

Amethyst's face was still in the covers. "A little bit warmer. At least we got their faces washed, even though it's probably undone now. Why can't their teacher pamper them?"

"She's afraid of them," said Miranda, sitting up. She sniffed. "Ewwwww! Oh, ewwww!" she moaned, holding her nose.

Amethyst sat up and made an identical face. "Disgusting," she said, plugging her nose.

The air smelled like someone had put lipstick, mouthwash, dirt, toothpaste, face cream, and hair into a bowl full of water, mixed it up, and spread it everywhere.

Amethyst didn't want to move from her bed, but she had to see what the terrors were doing now. She got up slowly, still holding her nose, and went into the bathroom.

She was horrified. Both the little girls' faces were completely covered in lipstick. They were using lipstick to draw on each other, even in their hair.

"Miranda," called Amethyst, even though it sounded like "Manda" with her nose plugged. "Be need to tabe conbrol." She snatched the lipsticks away from the monsters. Both of them screeched and yelped. Amethyst ignored them and put the lipsticks into Miranda's outstretched hand. "Pamper yourself," she ordered. "Try not to make a mess. I'll take care of them for now."

Emmy howled. "Why take my pink whip cream?"

"It's lipstick!" corrected Amethyst. Then she lunged at the girls and toppled on top of them. They fell into the bathtub, screaming and screeching the whole time.

Amethyst rolled her eyes and yanked their clothes off. "Bath time!"

But instead of yelping in glee, the two howled. "We *like* our makeup!" cried Rachel, trying to grab the lipstick smeared on her face.

"I know, I know," Amethyst said with annoyance. Then it came to her- the perfect solution!

"Miss Odelia doesn't like it!" she announced. "She told me if she sees such dirty little faces, she's going to punish you! *Severely!*"

Emmy's and Rachel's eyes grew wide with fright.

"Listen," ordered Amethyst, fighting back giggles. "You wash off this makeup, and I'll give you makeup you'll really enjoy- and something that Miss Odelia will like!"

"Yay!" cheered the little girls. "Okay, we'll do it."

Amethyst shut off the water and went back out to Miranda, who was putting the finishing touches on her lipstick. She told Miranda all about what had happened. Miranda laughed.

Amethyst was going back into the bathroom to start re-cleaning when there was a short, brisk knock at the door. They froze.

Then the door opened, and there was Victoria. "Is the bathroom ready?"

Miranda and Amethyst didn't say anything. They just stood there. Amethyst's hand was still outstretched towards the bathroom. Miranda had froze in the middle of closing the lipstick. They didn't move, just stood there, their eyes fixed on Victoria. They were both thinking the same thing: *It can't be time already.*

Victoria blinked. Then she nodded. "I see it's a no. Don't worry. I'll fix myself up in Mandy's bathroom, and don't worry, I won't tell."

Amethyst recovered from her stare. "Th-th-th-thanks."

"Amethyst, right?" Amethyst nodded.

Victoria smiled. "See you later. And did you hear- the inspector's coming?"

Yes, we heard," said Miranda, recovering also.

"It's going to be a while," she admitted. "Those monsters- Emmy and Rachel- still need to be 'pampered,' and Miranda and I

11

aren't even close to being done."

Victoria nodded. "I would help you, I really would, but I need to get myself fixed up. Miss Odelia's orders." She grimaced.

Amethyst nodded in understanding. "Better to have two girls not pampered than three."

Miranda had disappeared into the bathroom, and she now called, "Amethyst? We have a problem!"

As Victoria left the room, Amethyst turned slowly, afraid of what she would see.

"We have a leak!" announced Miranda with horror in her voice.

* * * * * * * * * * * * * * * * * * *

Miss Odelia carried Miranda in one hand and Amethyst in the other as she walked down the stairs. Amethyst was infuriated. She crossed her arms and glared at Miss Odelia.

Miss Odelia ignored the glare and brought them all the way down to the front entryway, where all the girls were lined up. The inspector was coming any second.

Miss Odelia thrust them into line. Miranda and Amethyst fell against the wall with the others roughly. Amethyst's face heated up, and she kept her arms angrily crossed. Her glare deepened. *How dare Miss Odelia carry us! And just because the room above us was careless enough to leak!*

Miss Odelia rummaged around in her purse until she found two bundles. She threw them at the girls. "Dress. Hurry."

Miranda and Amethyst did not need to be told twice, even in their anger. Since the inspector was coming they got to wear nice clothes. For once they did not even mind dressing in front of everyone else, even when Rachel and Emmy- who ended up needing to be dressed by Miss Odelia- teased and cried, "I see Amy's underpants!"

Finally they were dressed. They handed over their old

ragged clothes. Normally they got to keep the clothes they were given until they got ragged and torn.

A knock sounded at the door. Miss Odelia fluttered to it.

Before she swung it open, she said, "Now, girls, you know the rules. No teasing, no talking unless you are spoken to, and no telling this inspector the truth!" With that she swung open the door. Amethyst glared even harder, but then did her best to relax her glare when the door swung open.

"Miss Odelia, I presume?" the man offered his right hand.

"Mr. Jeremiah Chuckchester at your service." After he shook Miss Odelia's hand he gave a little bow. "And these are the lovely girls. It must be a thrill to stay here, Odelia, as they look full, warm, and satisfied."

Miss Odelia blushed. "Thank you. Now, Mr. Chuckchester, would you like to see the house?"

"Certainly," said Mr. Chuckchester, and he followed Miss Odelia towards the stairs. Jokingly, he added, "That's what I'm here for, is it not?"

Amethyst stepped up to Miss Odelia. She had to use all her willpower to keep her glare contained. If she could just go with on the inspection - sure, she'd miss the treats - but it would give her a chance to get back at Miss Odelia. It worked out perfectly; Miss Odelia would never dare scold her, nor punish her, while Mr. Chuckchester was there.

"Yes, what do you want, honey?" Miss Odelia turned and looked at Amethyst with fake sweetness in her eyes.

Amethyst bit back her anger and said in the sweetest voice she could manage, "Please, uh, Odelia, could I come with on the inspection?"

At the word 'Odelia' instead of 'Miss Odelia' Miss Odelia glared, but quickly diminished the glare. "Actually, sweetie, just me and Mr. Chuckchester are going to go this time. But if you need anything, sweet, just give a holler, alright?"

Amethyst replied with a snort and went back to her line.

As Miss Odelia left, Mrs. Vancolia approached them.

"Now, girls, would you like hot chocolate or hot tea with your cookies?"

Amethyst's mouth watered when she spotted the chocolate cookies in Mrs. Vancolia's hands. When Mrs. Vancolia handed her two big round cookies and a glass of hot chocolate, Amethyst just breathed in the scent. Ah, *cookies!* Ah, *chocolate!*

* * * * * * * * * * * * * * * * * * * *

An hour passed. Two hours. Three hours. Miss Odelia and Mr. Chuckchester did not return.

Amethyst was at the point where she didn't care. She had just eaten a filling dinner of hot fried chicken, sweet potatoes, green beans, crackers, cheese, corn, and fruit juice, and peaches for dessert. Now her stomach was full. She was also dressed in a warm, woven dress, with wool socks and clean Mary Jane shoes.

She thought about what she and Miranda had had to do.

They had not completed their work, really. They had managed to get Rachel and Emmy somewhat pretty, and the bathroom was fairly clean, but there was still the leak in the ceiling and the gobs of toothpaste on the floor. And they had to be pampered by none other than Miss Odelia!

Finally, footsteps sounded on the stairs and Miss Odelia, followed by Mr. Chuckchester, thundered down. "Darlings." Miss Odelia's voice was harsh. "Who caused the leak in room 20?"

Amethyst was confused; Miss Odelia had already known about the leak!

A smaller girl piped up. "Bathroom or room?"

"Bathroom," barked Miss Odelia. Then she seemed to remember she was supposed to be a nicey-nice lady. She apologized to the girl, and turned to Mr. Chuckchester.

Mr. Chuckchester was frowning. "You're sure it was one of these girls?"

Miss Odelia started to say "Yes" but instead caught herself and said, "Oh, um, I'm not sure of anything. These girls are such adorable little angels they wouldn't possibly do such a bad thing."

"Yes," agreed Mr. Chuckchester, looking thoughtful. "But

you know it's possible the leak wasn't made by your little angels here. The building could be leaking by itself. Do you keep the upstairs in good order on a daily basis? Do you do the plumbing checks monthly? I noticed a few pipes were cracked in the basement and that you have a leak down there also."

Amethyst sucked in her breath. Miss Odelia had a plumber come in as often as she kissed the girls. In other words, never.

And the upstairs was in horrible shape besides. Once, in one room, the ceiling plaster had started to fall onto the girl below, and instead of hiring a ceiling-fixer, all Miss Odelia did was tape it up with piles of duct tape! Another time, the roof in one room had caved in and Miss Odelia had just taped covering on the roof where the hole was. There was still a nasty hole, Amethyst heard.

Miss Odelia looked at a loss for words. *She's afraid to lie,* realized Amethyst.

She was suddenly struck with an idea. Was it worth it? Yes, if Mr. Chuckchester believed her. True, Miss Odelia had forbidden it. But if Amethyst was going to do it, what better time but now, when Miss Odelia was at a loss for words?

She took a deep breath and opened her mouth. In a loud, clear, brave tone she said:

"No. Mr. Chuckchester, she *doesn't*. She *hates* us, too, and she wouldn't care if we all suddenly got sick with a life-threatening disease." Her voice grew angry, and every single other girl at the asylum joined her in shouting the truth, not saying it from memory but from anger, and they said the exact same words only because it was the same thing every single girl was thinking. They chanted, even Amethyst, in a loud angry tone, "She's just tricking you. We are barely fed. We are barely clothed. We barely survive here!"

Mr. Chuckchester's eyes grew red and blazing. He turned to Miss Odelia, clearly believing the girls.

"You lied," he hissed in a snake-like tone, then he grabbed her arm roughly and forced her towards the front door.

chapter three
Amethyst's Punishments

Amethyst." Miss Odelia tapped her desk with her ruler.

"You are in *severe* trouble." Her voice rose. "How *dare* you reveal the true identity of the asylum to Mr. Jeremiah Chuckchester? How *dare* you!"

"I.... needed him to see," said Amethyst boldly, looking at Miss Odelia with fiery eyes. But still she wobbled in fear, and her breath came in short gasps.

She thought shakily about the previous night. Mr. Chuckchester had attempted to drag Miss Odelia to the door, but he was no match for the other officials at the asylum. Then they had glared at him and made him swear not to tell a soul. Miss Odelia told him if he did, he would regret it. Or, in her own words, he would "*severely* regret it."

Mr. Chuckchester had mumbled he wouldn't and stumbled out of the asylum holding his hat. He had not come back.

And now, a day later, Amethyst was being punished for starting the whole thing. And boy was she scared!

"I'm sorry, Miss Odelia," she finally said, although she didn't mean it. Not At All.

Miss Odelia somehow could tell this. "Hm. It seems to be I need to make you sorry for real. What about, oh, perhaps a whipping?"

Amethyst shook her head violently. "No, ma'am," she said, and bobbed a elegant curtsy.

"Oh?" said Miss Odelia. "What will fix you then?" Then, without waiting for an answer, she said, "Will a day in the cellar fix you?"

"No-" started Amethyst, but she was cut off by a voice in the doorway. Amethyst swirled and saw a very fat lady with chubby fingers grasping a parasol, and with sinking heart recognized her as Mrs. Vancolia.

"Yes, it will," said the very fat teacher. "If you send her down with some schoolbooks, she'll learn all she needs to. I can quiz her when she returns."

"Excellent idea," commented Miss Odelia. "Girl, get in the cellar."

"Please," begged Amethyst. She got down on her scraped little knees and looked up at Miss Odelia. "*Please!*"

Miss Odelia rolled her eyes and grabbed Amethyst's wrists. "You could've done it the easy way, but I guess you chose the hard way." Amethyst struggled, but soon she felt Mrs. Vancolia's chubby fingers on her ankles and she was lifted off the ground. She let out a small cry. She was brought down to the cellar and books were toppled on top of her.

Three days and nights came and went. All Amethyst could do was sit and think. (She had, of course, taken the chance and *not* done any schoolwork.) She sat all day, crouched in the cellar corner, trying to block out the sound of the *drip drop* coming from behind the cellar freezer, from which Amethyst was getting all her food because Mrs. Vancolia never brought down any food. There was no water in the freezer, but there was ice, so whenever Amethyst got thirsty she would find an ice cube and suck on it until it melted away.

But now, two days after being thrown down, the food began to run out.

Amethyst scavenged the freezer top to bottom, but all she could find were ice cubes, ice cubes and more ice cubes. Well, at least she wouldn't die from thirst. How long was it you could go without food? A month? Surely Mrs. Vancolia would come down before a month was up! After that realization Amethyst relaxed a little more. When she got brought up, she would try to behave so she could get a good meal.

On the third day, Amethyst was sitting in the damp, dark cellar with a zillion cobwebs around her, with her stomach growling and rumbling, when suddenly the cellar door flew open. Mrs. Vancolia was there. She shuffled lazily down the stairs, grabbed Amethyst's wrist, and tugged her up. Amethyst closed her eyes, relieved to breathe fresh air and not the damp air that was in the cellar.

But when she opened her eyes, she wished she still had them closed.

Once every few months, the orphan train stopped at the asylum and picked up around forty girls to take, except this train wasn't the train that brought orphans to kind, loving families. That was just the name. This train came only to take girls off Miss Odelia's hands. To make things easier for her. To rid her of the girls.

Sometimes the train dropped girls off at wealthy families' homes to be slaves. Sometimes they just left them on the side of the road. And there were rumors going around that sometimes the girls were locked in dark boxcars.

And now that would all happen to Amethyst.

Mrs. Vancolia pushed Amethyst roughly into one of the lines. "Line up!" she snapped, and went to chat with Miss Odelia.

Amethyst did as she was told, looking out into the broad daylight, perhaps the last time she'd ever see it.

Just then, from the back of the room, voices rose. Every head turned. Miss Odelia and Mrs. Vancolia were leaving the room. Amethyst heard snitches of their argument.

Then the realization dawned on every girl in the place. The whole area had *no adults*. Only *girls!*

Amethyst spotted a few girls running to escape out of the asylum's doors. Some simply hid behind desks and decorations. The rest stayed, too afraid to do anything. Amethyst considered, her heart pounding. Could she escape? If she ran out of those doors... they were only a few feet away.... she would be free...

If she were free, who would take care of her?

She made her decision. Just as Miss Odelia re-entered the room, she ducked down behind a tall decorative tree. She hoped nobody had seen her, but it was too late.

chapter four
All Aboard the Orphan Train!

Miss Odelia, of them all, had seen her. She went over calmly to Amethyst and grabbed her dress, ripping it. Amethyst blinked back tears. "Why do you do this?" she cried. "Why are you so mean?"

"You'd better line up," was all Miss Odelia said. "Line up or you'll be *severely* punished!"

Amethyst did as she was told. She was getting sick of the *severelys*.

A train whistle sounded from far off. It was shrill and clear. Miss Odelia flew into a panic. "Oh my!" she gasped to Mrs. Vancolia. "The train's about here and we still have ten brats to collect!"

Mrs. Vancolia looked at her curiously. "Are any of them......"

Miss Odelia shook her head firmly. "I don't think so."

Amethyst was puzzled. What did Mrs. Vancolia mean by *Are any of them...?*

"Okay, then, we'll just not board them. If none of them are...." -she stopped suddenly, realizing Amethyst was eavesdropping. "Well, you know what I mean."

Miss Odelia glared in Amethyst's direction and nodded at Mrs. Vancolia. "I suppose you're right, Penelope."

Penelope was Mrs. Vancolia's first name?

"Oh, and that reminds me," said Miss Odelia lazily, casting a triumphant look in Amethyst's direction, "we ought to tie 'em up before they can escape. Help me."

Amethyst panicked. *What were they going to do? Tie them up so tightly they couldn't breathe?*

Fortunately Miss Odelia just tied Amethyst's ankle to the girl ahead of her. "We won't have anyone escaping," she told her. "Now, girls. Get. Going!"

Amethyst and the others were shuffled forward out the doors, down the drive, around the corner, and to the train. Amethyst wished she had run out the doors while she had the chance. She could see some of the kids a little bit away, casually walking and looking like they had somewhere to go. Amethyst felt relief as nobody saw them.

"All aboard!" called a sharp voice. "All aboard the orphan-train!"

The train suddenly blew its whistle again, causing all the girls to cover their ears in disgust. Unfortunately, it did no good.

Miss Odelia herded the children onto the train. They took as small steps as possible, wanting to delay the moment as long as they could, until Miss Odelia hissed at them, "Be quiet and *move faster!* Get seated! On the double!"

Amethyst sighed a long, trembly sigh as the rope on her ankle was cut and she was pushed roughly into a window seat. She sat down and sighed again. It would've been nice if she could sit with somebody, but Miss Odelia didn't put any other girl in the seat next to her. Well, at least she'd have room to stretch out.

She thought for a second. The train had come before, that much was true, but never for *her.* Didn't Miss Odelia know her mother was coming back for her? Why did she put her on this train?

Amethyst gazed out the window sadly. The window was covered in grime and someone had drawn a small smiley-face in it. Amethyst blinked back tears and drew her own smiley-face next to it.

"I get this seat!"

A familiar voice startled Amethyst out of her thoughts. She turned and groaned.

"No, I get it! You always get the best stuff! I want something good for a change!" whined Emmy to her twin Rachel.

"Girls!" yelled Miss Odelia. "Sit down or I'll be forced to tie you down."

"But... Miss Odelia, she always gets the best stuff!" whined Emmy. "Can I get the window this time?"

"NO!" screamed Miss Odelia. "Whatever-your-name is, the one who just talked, sit down. Your twin will get the window."

"Fine," muttered Emmy. Rachel shot her a triumphant glance.

Why were Emmy and Rachel on this train?

Amethyst looked through the grime and saw the landscape sitting still outside. Though she was happy it hadn't started (she wanted to delay the moment as long as possible), she was curious of *why* it hadn't started; normally the train zoomed off as soon as every kid was boarded.

Just then she heard the *creeak* of the automatic train door and Miss Odelia stepped out, and then onto the train came the ugliest woman Amethyst had ever seen. As Amethyst watched, the ugly lady muttered something to the conductor, and then started to walk down the aisle, scaring the children more.

When she got to Emmy and Rachel, she grinned and said, "You're sure ugly ones."

"Are not!" said Emmy bravely. "You the ugly one."

"Nah," said the lady, smiling wickedly. "This is a pretty scary train. You know what happens if-"

Amethyst had heard enough. She jumped out of her seat. She may not be fond of Emmy and Rachel but they were the only people she knew on this train and she wasn't about to let them be tortured.

"Stop it!" she yelled at the woman, and punched her in the nose.

The lady screeched for a second, but then pinched her nose softly and in a second looked normal again.

Amethyst backed up, terrified, and looked at the woman.

She had a triangular face with piercing red eyes. Her hair was sticking up in an odd angle, and it was a blackish color with streaks of greenish pinkish. Her face displayed sharp curves instead of elegant ones. Her lips were black and her mouth had a half-frown half-smile look.

"A fighter," mused the lady. "Good, good." She eyed Amethyst. "What is your name, ugly one?"

"Amethyst," said Amethyst without thinking. "Amethyst Butternut."

"And what are your two friends' names?" she asked, gesturing to Emmy and Rachel.

"Emmy and Rachel."

"Last names?" The lady's voice became low and raspy.

"I..... I.... I don't know."

"Fine," said the lady, her eyes getting fiery. She took Amethyst by the wrist. "Come with me."

Amethyst didn't bother to struggle. She knew it'd do no good.

* * * * * * * * * * * * * * * *

The lady brought her through cars, cars, and more cars until they reached a damp, dark boxcar that had access from either end. The lady tossed Amethyst into the boxcar like she was a rag doll and yelled, "FREEZE!" Then she cackled and left the boxcar. Suddenly Amethyst could no longer move.

How did she do that? wondered Amethyst. *Fairies didn't exist. Is she making me think I'm frozen when I'm not?* She tried moving.

Nope, the magic- or whatever it was- was real.

"What's your name?" came a voice from the dark. If she hadn't been frozen, Amethyst would've jumped.

The voice seemed to sense her cautiousness. "It's okay, I'm frozen too. My name's Angelica," said the voice.

Amethyst strained her eyes to see Angelica, but it was too dark.

"Are you the only one here?" she asked.

"No," said Angelica. "Emily's on your right, McKenna's on your left, and Courtney's right between me and McKenna, and I'm in front of you."

Amethyst could picture it. "I'm Amethyst," she finally said. "How long have you been here?"

"That's a really pretty name," came a voice from her right.

Must be Emily, thought Amethyst.

"We've been here, oh, a few months," said Angelica.

"*Months!*" Amethyst was horrified. "How do you survive?"

"Eugenia unfreezes us three times a day to give us bread and beans," said a voice that must've been Courtney's.

"Oh. Is she a fairy or something? I mean, she can freeze us," said Amethyst, correctly guessing Eugenia was the lady who had thrown her into the boxcar.

Angelica paused. "I'm pretty sure she's an evil fairy."

An evil fairy! Amethyst shuddered. "I didn't know they existed."

A new voice came, "Me neither, until she froze me." It had to have been McKenna's.

"But...." Amethyst didn't want to be hurtful. "What proof do you have she's an evil fairy? Besides the fact she can freeze us?"

"Well....." Angelica hesitated. "She can do other things. Freaky, creepy things."

"Like what?" asked Amethyst gently.

"Well, she can get a flame on a candle by just snapping her fingers, and she can fly. She can create fireworks by snapping her fingers, and she can do any magic she likes," said Angelica. "She has a wand, too," added McKenna proudly.

Amethyst didn't want to think about all those things

24

anymore, so she changed the subject. "So, how'd you all get here?" she asked, as if it was a perfectly normal day and they were having a perfectly normal conversation.

"I'll tell how *I* got here," said McKenna, rudely. "One day I was taking a nice walk down the road to my grandmama's house, when suddenly this big train pulls up, and this big *fat* lady-"

"Whoa there, McKenna!" cried Courtney. "I think you're getting a little carried away! Eugenia isn't big nor fat!"

"Did I *say* it was Eugenia?" asked McKenna angrily. "No! I said it was an big fat lady! Well, anyway, this big, fat lady steps out of the train, and she comes to me, and of course I'm just scared out of my wits, so I just start running, and this lady just says, 'Stop right there, little girl!' and suddenly I'm frozen. And-"

"I thought you said it *wasn't* Eugenia," said Courtney with much annoyance.

"Haven't you heard this story before?" cried Angelica.

"No," said Courtney. "I was sleeping when McKenna told it, and afterword I wasn't interested."

"Please go on, McKenna," said Amethyst.

McKenna smiled, although it was not visible in the dim light. She went on.

"So, I just start yelling, but this big, fat lady just came over and picked me up, and that causes me to drop my basket of cookies for my grandmama, which I had been taking to her because she was sick-"

"This sounds a bit too much like Little Red Riding Hood to me," interrupted Courtney. "You're *sure* you're not making this up, McKenna?"

"Positive!" insisted McKenna. "So, anyway, I'm just too scared to do anything, so I just come with the big, fat lady who says her name is Eugenia. And I get thrown in here. Oh, and my *poor* grandmama never, *ever* got her cookies. The end!"

"It's nice," said Amethyst, because she couldn't think of anything else to say to such an explanation, "but didn't you say it *wasn't* Eugenia?"

Angelica smiled. "Eugenia's mom's name was Eugenia, too, and that's who McKenna's referring to," she explained.

"Wait," said Amethyst. "You said her mom's name *was* Eugenia, not her mom's name *is* Eugenia. Did she die?"

"Yep," said Angelica, grinning widely. "She fell off a moving train, and *bam!* Just like that, she's gone!"

Amethyst smiled.

"I can go next," volunteered Emily, "because my story is boring. Angelica and I were thrown in here together, a little after McKenna, who was the first. You see, we'd just came from an asylum, and we were best friends. We managed to get seats together on the train. By this time, it's not Eugenia's mom; it's Eugenia. So she takes us and throws us in here for no reason at all."

"That *is* boring," commented McKenna.

"McKenna!" scolded Courtney. "That's rude!" Then she cleared her throat. "Is anybody interested in *my* story? How *I* got here?"

"No," said McKenna.

"Yes," said Amethyst kindly.

Courtney shot McKenna an angry look and started.

"Well.... I was living at this really bad asylum," she said, rather quietly, "and I really had no friends there, except for one girl I sometimes hung out with. And then one day the orphan train was coming and the headmistress put me on. And then Eugenia threw me in here. I'm the most recent arrival," she added. "I arrived-"

But before she could finish thundering footsteps sounded outside the boxcar. They came closer, and closer and closer.

chapter five
Blowing
Misadventures

The lady that had thrown Amethyst in the boxcar entered, swinging open the door and filling the windowless boxcar with sunny daylight. To Amethyst it felt like her eyes had been closed and she had only just opened them. She basked in the sunny light.

All too soon, however, the lady closed the boxcar. Amethyst whimpered, but then the lady reached up and pulled a string, making one single lightbulb light up.

Whoa, next times she freezes me, if I stand up, we'll get some light if I can pull the string before she says "Freeze", thought Amethyst happily.

The lady handed out plates of unbuttered bread, a lump of cheese and soggy black beans. As she was doing this she said,

"For the ugly one that doesn't know, my name's Eugenia."

So I was right, thought Amethyst.

"So, I'm not ugly, only her?" McKenna asked hopefully.

Eugenia considered. "No, you are ugly, maybe even more so. By the way, you can unfreeze now."

Amethyst took a deep breath of relief as she found she could move again. Even though the bread was rather moldy, she took a bite, and soon it was all gone. Eugenia handed her a glass of water and she drank it down in one gulp.

When everyone was finished, Eugenia gathered the plates and turned off the light. Amethyst remembered her idea and stood up, along with the others. As Eugenia opened her mouth to shout, "Freeze," Amethyst pulled the string and as the boxcar door banged shut, the car stayed light.

Amethyst's plan had worked. Her hand was frozen on the light string, that much was true, but at least they wouldn't be sitting in the dark.

"Whoa," said Angelica. "Good job, Amethyst."

"Yea," echoed McKenna. "Good job."

Courtney squinted. "We can actually see each other!" She made it sound like a miracle, and in a way, it was.

Amethyst studied them. McKenna was wearing a drab brown dress and a scarf around her head like a headband, tied in a sloppy bow. She had tangled brown hair and blue eyes.

Angelica was wearing similar to McKenna's but she didn't have a headband, and her dress was a dark bluish.

Amethyst frowned. "You know Eugenia better than I do. Would she punish me if she saw I found a way to get the light on?"

Emily attempted a shrug. "You never know. She might think you are denying her magic by being unfrozen when she froze you, and and then that could probably get bad."

Unaffected by the freezing magic, her blonde hair flowed gently around her shoulders.

"Like.... what would happen?" stammered Amethyst fearfully.

"Well," said Courtney, who had bright green eyes, freckles, and brown hair, "I suppose she would, oh, maybe make us not talk or something. Or maybe she'd tie you down. Anyway, it'd be pretty bad. I just know."

Amethyst said worriedly, "Okay, then, I need to get on the ground. And you need to, too."

"How?" asked Angelica.

Amethyst glanced around the room. "Maybe... blown down?"

"Wouldn't that hurt?" said Emily.

"Sure, I guess. But according to Courtney, it'd be a lot better than Eugenia's wrath."

Courtney's cheeks flushed.

"How will we- aha! The door!" announced Emily proudly.

They all looked. It looked like a regular boxcar door.

"It's a bit open," said Emily.

They looked again and saw it was indeed true.

"Eugenia must've slammed it too hard," said McKenna.

"It's a start," admitted Angelica, "but it's not everything. Any ideas on how to get a door from being a crack open to being fully open so the wind can blow us over?"

McKenna frowned. "That will be rather hard, you see, Angelica, because apparently we can't move."

"That's kind of obvious, McKenna," said Courtney.

"That's it!" said McKenna. "I've got an idea!" She quickly explained her idea, which was to blow as hard as they could, until the door swung open.

Suddenly Amethyst found a disappointing detail. "How," she said, "will we explain to Eugenia how the door got open?"

McKenna had an answer. "We just suck in our breath very quickly," she said, "and the door will swing shut!"

"Oh boy," groaned Emily. "McKenna, that's not going to work."

"Well, okay!" said McKenna cheerfully. "Does anyone have any better ideas?" Nobody did, so they ended up trying out McKenna's ridiculous idea.

"Blow!" McKenna commanded. "Blow, blow, blow!"

As she blew, Amethyst noticed McKenna reminded her a lot of Emmy and Rachel. Where were the two monsters now? Were they still on this very train?

They blew until Amethyst started to feel dizzy, and despite being frozen the dizziness took over and she fell backwards.

"Uhhhh," she groaned.

In a minute her friends had joined her, dizzy and faint, but soon they regained steadiness and started to talk. "McKenna did have a good idea," praised Emily, "although it didn't work the way she was planning!" Everyone giggled.

* * * * * * * * * * * * * * * * * * * *

Days went by slowly and they developed a routine. Sleep, unfreeze, eat breakfast, freeze. Sit around, unfreeze, lunch, freeze. Sit around, unfreeze, dinner, freeze. Sit around, unfreeze, get in sleeping position, freeze.

During long days they played games, like Twenty Questions and games where they told stories. They attempted to play telephone but were rarely successful. Slowly Amethyst got sick of beans and bread. That's all it was. Beans and bread, beans and bread.

Amethyst slowly adjusted to her new life. She had given up escaping because Angelica told her McKenna had tried it before and had been severely punished. Deep deep down, though, Amethyst wanted to escape. She dreamed about it- Eugenia going to the bathroom during eating hours and spending a long time (she did do that, miraculously, but no one dared to escape, as the train was moving and Eugenia would catch them in no time); Amethyst and Angelica and the others jumping off the train; running and running to a safe place, and never getting caught. Every morning Amethyst would wake up, and utter a saddening sigh that the dream were only a dream and not true.

* * * * * * * * * * * * * * * * * * * *

In a small city not far away called Glazings, Mary Littles sat up, awake, in the middle of the night. She was in her small house in her bedroom, all alone. The room next to her sat empty and vacant, meant for her children. Her heart ached for what could never be. It kept her awake nearly every night until at least 1 a.m, when she would hear the shrill whistle of a train screeching by. She wished things were different, but alas; she was stuck owning a tiny shop on the edge of town.

chapter six
Meeting Mary

One morning, Amethyst was just waking up when Eugenia swung open the boxcar door and switched on the light. It had been a week since the blowing misadventures.

Eugenia, as always, was holding five plates and five cups, and handed them each a plate. Amethyst sighed inwardly, desperately despising the dreaded beans and bread.

Eugenia cleared her throat. "Ahem. Breakfast." She added "Unfreeze", and smiled as she handed out the plates of food.

"Enjoy this meal, it might be your last!"

Amethyst was utterly terrified. A spark of courage arose inside her, and without thinking, threw her plate of food at Eugenia.

As Amethyst had hoped, Eugenia was too startled to think about grabbing her wand. Amethyst took the chance and attacked her, not minding that beans got slathered all over her dress. After a quick scuffle Amethyst found herself being pushed from the train as the others looked on in horror. For once even McKenna was quiet.

Eugenia dusted off her hands. "That's taken care of. One less bratty child to worry about." Giving the horrified girls a final wicked grin, she gathered up the food plates, muttered a "freeze" and exited the boxcar.

* * * * * * * * * * * * * * * * * * *

Outside the boxcar, Amethyst fell onto the grass and rolled violently end over end a few times before she finally came to a stop.

Dazed, she opened her eyes and just stared at the sky for a while. *Where am I? What just happened?* Then it slowly came back to her.

She finally sat up, not believing her luck. She moved each part of her body carefully; luckily nothing seemed broken. Her ankle did feel a little sprained but that was it. But she had *escaped!* Well, in a way. But she had! "I'm free, I'm free!" she called into the blowing wind.

But then it struck her. This was no time to be excited for herself; she had to get help for her friends- and everyone on the train, for that matter. She had to find out where the train was going next. Then she could try to help.

She looked around, finding herself in the middle of a busy city. *Finding someone should be no problem,* she thought. Standing up carefully, she limped across the train tracks and headed down the side of the busy street. There was a supermarket ahead of her, but she wanted to find a smaller store, where'd there be less people. Her story was rather unbelievable for anybody who had not been there, and she didn't want to attract lots of people. She walked for a bit, and then saw a small shop called Mary's Place in the middle of a strip mall. She walked inside, wondering what kind of store it was.

It was an office store. On one side of the store she saw staplers and printer paper, and on the other side pens and rulers and Expo markers.

The lady behind the counter spotted her. Slowly Amethyst

walked over to the counter. She saw first doubt in the lady's eyes, then amazement, then finally joyfulness. *Maybe I'm the first customer she's ever had,* thought Amethyst. *Well, she's out of luck, I've come for help, not office supplies.*

The lady came out from behind the counter and wrapped her arms around Amethyst. Amethyst stood like a statue, her eyes wide and flashing. *Why was this stranger* hugging *her?*

"Little girl," said the lady, backing away. Then she gasped. "What happened to you?"

Amethyst, hoping it didn't sound ridiculous, explained everything, from Miss Odelia to finally being thrown off the train. Surprisingly, the lady didn't seem surprised. She just nodded as if that sort of stuff happened all the time.

"So," ended Amethyst, "I need to rescue my friends before it's too late."

The lady, who said her name was Mary, replied, "Well, I don't know what we can do, but what if I take you first to my house, to tidy you up, and then to the train station?"

"Uh...." Amethyst didn't want to sound ungrateful. "Can we, uh, help my friends first?"

Mary paused, looking at Amethyst's bruised ankle, but then she nodded. "I guess, but just let me wrap your ankle when we get to the train station."

"Fine," said Amethyst.

Mary disappeared into the back room, and came out with a large gauze bandage. She brought Amethyst out of the store, changed the shop's sign to CLOSED, and locked the door behind her. Then they went to Mary's car.

Amethyst hesitated before getting into the car. Mary saw her hesitation. "What's wrong?"

"Nothing," said Amethyst, her cheeks flushing. "It's just..... I know this sounds silly.... but I've never been in a car before." It was true. Until that awful day she boarded the orphan train, as far as she could remember, she had never been outside the asylum's walls.

Mary laughed, although it was a faint sort of laugh. "Buckle up, little girl, because now you're in one. What did you say your name was again?"

Amethyst hesitated.

"It's okay," reassured Mary. "I won't hurt you."

"My name's Amethyst," Amethyst said. "Amethyst Butternut."

Mary swallowed. "I like your name."

"Thanks." No adult had ever commented on her name.

Finally they reached the train station. Amethyst did not like riding in the car, she discovered, and was happy to get out.

After she bound Amethyst's ankle, Mary picked up a newsletter labeled ORPHAN TRAIN. She read, "Orphan train: first stop, Asylum Odelia." She turned to Amethyst. "Should we-"

"That's the one I used to live in," said Amethyst. She looked at the newsletter and pointed to another name. "Asylum Quiana is the one we want." At least, Amethyst was pretty sure it was.

"Okay," said Mary obediently. She flashed Amethyst a quizzical look. "It's a few miles from here. Want me to drive you?"

"Yes, please," said Amethyst, remembering her manners.

She was getting excited. If all went well, she'd see her friends again in a few hours. She missed all of them already, even though she had seen them only that morning. Angelica, the leader; Emily, the shy but smart one; McKenna, the one who always made her laugh; and Courtney, the motherly one.

She missed every single one of them. And- and- for some reason she missed Emmy and Rachel, too. Even though they were The Most Annoying Kids On The Planet, she missed them.

In the car, Amethyst was struck with an idea. "Mary?" she asked timidly, "do you.... do you think you can help me?" She knew the answer would be no, but she asked anyway.

But to her surprise, Mary said, "Sure, honey cake. There's a first time for everything, after all!" *Honey cake.* Where had she heard that before?

"Besides, I know it's true," added Mary, "and since it is, it must be stopped." Amethyst thought she heard Mary mutter, "At least I hope we can do this."

The rest of the short ride Amethyst's mind was filled with worry. *What if the train had already got there and left? What if they couldn't rescue the girls? What if Eugenia had done something bad to the others?*

She must've looked worried, because Mary told her, "It'll be fine, Amethyst." They drove into the parking lot, got out and walked into Asylum Quiana.

chapter seven
Asylum Quiana

A lady with a false smile greeted them.

"Hello, ma'am," she said. "What can I do for you today? I am Miss Quiana, head of this asylum." She completely ignored Amethyst.

"I need you to cancel the orphan train's stop here," said Mary.

"Why?"

"Because I said so."

"Are you adopting them all?" asked Miss Quiana curiously.

She reminds me an awful lot of Miss Odelia, thought Amethyst.

"No." Mary looked triumphant. "I am the President of Orphan Asylums."

"There's no such thing," said Miss Quiana quickly.

"There is too." It was funny to see adults fighting. "The people of this city decided the orphan-train thingy was going a bit too far, so they hired me to settle it."

Amethyst wondered if Mary was lying or telling the truth.

As the adults argued, Amethyst let her gaze wander around

the dimly lit asylum. It was almost identical to hers - bare walls, grimy floors, creaky slanted stairs that were a challenge to walk up, tall ceilings. Classrooms with peeling wood by the door frames, and broken railings, and signs everywhere declaring the rules and the punishments.

"What are you gonna do about it, huh?" said Miss Quiana.

"I am going to tell you to cancel the orphan train's stop. Cancel the orphan train's stop, Quiana."

"Miss Quiana," corrected Miss Quiana harshly.

"Yes, of course," said Mary calmly.

Miss Quiana paused, and considered all that Mary had said. "What do I do with the orphans, then?"

"I know lots of people who would be happy to adopt them," said Mary. She turned to the frightened children, who had gathered to see the commotion. "By the end of this week, you all will have a home- and siblings will not be split apart, mind you."

Everyone cheered.

But the excitement was cut short by a scream coming from the other side of the building.

"WHAT'S THAT?" snapped Mary.

"Just Lucy," said Miss Quiana, acting as if Lucy were a broom or a mop. "I had to punish her, because all she does all day is cry, cry, cry. She's six years old and a little nuisance."

"What did you do?" Mary's voice was harsh.

"Locked her up in the back room," said Miss Quiana, as if locking orphans up was something everyone did.

"Give me the key," Mary snapped.

"You didn't adopt her," was Miss Quiana's excuse.

"I don't care," said Mary. "Come on, kids." She ran down the hallway to the back room with Amethyst and the others at her heels.

Since Miss Quiana didn't give Mary the key, Mary banged on the door until it fell in.

A small girl, dressed in rags, stood in the door. She had long, smooth golden red hair and beautiful blue eyes. She was crying.

"Are you okay, Lucy?" asked Mary softly.

Lucy shook her small head. "I'm so hungry," she said. "I only had a piece of bread for breakfast, and it's past lunch!"

Despite their situation, Mary had to giggle a little at the little girl's explanation of how much food she had had. But she said, "Poor girl!"

"Poor girl, huh?" asked Miss Quiana. "Well, she's the one girl who you won't adopt- or anyone else, for that matter."

She grabbed Lucy roughly by her wrist.

Lucy, tears streaming down her cheeks, screamed.

"You let her go," Mary said. She nudged Amethyst. "Get to the station. I'll take care of this mess."

Amethyst, knowing that Mary really meant, 'Go to the train station and wait for the train and I'll be out soon so we can rescue your friends', ran outside, beckoning for the others to follow.

"We're not going on the train, are we?" a young girl asked.

"No," said Amethyst. "We're fighting." She explained the evil fairy Eugenia to the children. Some of them were frightened, but others were brave and ready.

"Some of us are going to go to the boxcars, and break in. Inside there's frozen girls, frozen by Eugenia, an evil fairy. Please help these girls out. Once they exit the boxcar the magic ends. The rest of us, meanwhile, will be attacking the passenger cars. We need to get everyone there on our side. Then come help the rest of us- we'll be attacking the evil fairy. Everyone got it?"

"Yes," they said, in unison.

Just then, a train whistle sounded.

"Here it comes!" shouted Amethyst to the group.

The train pulled up.

The train conductor leaned out the window. "Where's Miss Quiana?" he growled.

Amethyst started to shout, "Somewhere," but Miss Quiana thundered out, dragging Lucy behind her and pushing the children aside. Mary followed, looking defeated.

Uh, oh, thought Amethyst. *Miss Quiana must have won that battle!* She winced.

"Right here," Miss Quiana said.

The conductor grinned evilly down at poor Lucy and

cackled. "*That's* the brat? Okay, bring her down to boxcar number twenty four, and I'll see she's treated right."

Miss Quiana saluted, tightened her grip on Lucy and trudged down to boxcar twenty-four, which Amethyst recognized as the one she'd been captive on. Oh, she just couldn't let Lucy be there! It would be... torture for the poor girl! Amethyst looked away and hoped this attack would work.

Amethyst knew she should be fighting, but she couldn't help it. She needed to see if her friends were alright.

Please, please, have the girls be unfrozen, she thought.

"Door's locked!" yelled a boy near the boxcar. He tugged on the door. "Locked!"

Locked. It couldn't be! Amethyst ran up, pushing the boy aside. She pulled the door and groaned.

Then the door flew open. The children around it scattered, all but Amethyst. She just smiled.

Angelica came running out. "You're just in time!" she yelled. "We're unfrozen for food, and Eugenia just went to the bathroom!"

Amethyst helped Angelica and the others down. Angelica hugged Amethyst.

The boy who yelled "door's locked" looked on in disgust.

"Girls, girls, sorry to stop the reunion, but we've got to get going. That evil fairy'll be back soon, if that girl isn't lying."

"I'm not lying!" Angelica practically yelled.

"What's your name, liar?" The boy grinned. "I'm Josh."

"Doesn't matter to you," growled Angelica.

Amethyst laughed and stepped between them. "Angelica, Josh's right. Let's get a move on!"

"A move on, a move on, a move on," chanted McKenna happily.

"That's right," called Amethyst. "Let's go, troops!"

"Wait a second," called Courtney, trailing behind them. "We aren't doing this just because McKenna started chanting, right?" Amethyst sighed.

"Hey, you never told me what your name was," said Josh, tagging along behind the fast-walking Amethyst.

"I'm Amethyst," Amethyst said.

Mary noticed the troops and named herself head of the army.

"Okay, troops, follow me!" She proudly began to march away.

But Mary had forgotten one person.

Eugenia came barging out of boxcar 24. She laughed a great big laugh and all the children scattered. She laughed another big laugh and snapped her fingers. "Freeze!"

All was silent.

And then came McKenna's voice. "Well, this is awkward."

chapter eight
Back on the Dismal Train

Amethyst looked around in a panic. Was everyone okay? Had anyone escaped? No. Everyone was frozen, and the fact they were alright *now* was completely besides the point. All Eugenia had to do was snap her fingers or wave her wand and they could be anything *but* alright.

Lucy, who had no idea whatsoever what was going on, said in a loud voice, "Could someone please say 'Unfreeze'?"

"Unfreeze," came McKenna's voice again. "Uh-oh, looks like only Ugly Eugenia has powers, not me." Small giggles echoed across the ocean of children.

Eugenia rolled her eyes and pushed her way through the crowd until she came to Mary. Mary winced, as if she was embarrassed by the fact she was frozen.

"Let me get this straight," said Eugenia. "You surrendered."

Surrendered? Eugenia doesn't even know who Mary is! Then

Amethyst reconsidered. *Or does she?*

Mary winced again. "I did not, and I never intend to."

"If you don't surrender, all these poor children will be under my control....."

"I will never surrender. Besides, they'll be in your control either way."

"So they're mine?"

"No," said Mary. "What I mean is you will let the children go without me surrendering."

Eugenia laughed nervously. "Well-"

"Great. Glad this worked out," said Mary.

Eugenia's eyes glistened with anger, but she did nothing.

She reluctantly started away. She walked right up to Miss Quiana, who was not frozen somehow, and said, "Which one is it?"

Miss Quiana pointed to Lucy, who was lying on the ground. "There's the brat," she said.

Why is Lucy so important to Eugenia and Miss Quiana? wondered Amethyst.

Eugenia touched Lucy. "Unfreeze," she said.

Lucy stood up and tried to run, but Eugenia blocked her way. "Should I freeze you again?" she threatened. Lucy's eyes widened. She shook her head violently, then let Eugenia walk around her twice. Then Eugenia grabbed Lucy's hand and led her to the train. On her way, she touched Amethyst's arm and dragged her too. Amethyst bumped along, being frozen still.

Eugenia dragged them onto the train, despite their tries to flee, threw them into a seat, and said, "Freeze." Then she disappeared out the door.

Outside, Lucy and Amethyst heard her say,

"UNFREEZE!"

Then onto the train came Angelica, Emily, Courtney, McKenna, Mary, and Josh. Outside, the children were being ushered back into the asylum.

The train blasted its whistle and started.

* *

Amethyst wished she could scoot along the seat and sit next to Mary, but she was frozen still. Her stomach rumbled. She hadn't had anything to eat since Eugenia had given her bread yesterday night. Was it really only yesterday night? she wondered. It seems like years ago. The next time Eugenia came in, Mary looked her in the eye and told her unfreeze them.

Eugenia replied, "No way."

"Please," begged Lucy with tears in her eyes. "Please, Miss Eugenia!"

No one had ever called Eugenia "miss" before. She couldn't stand it. She yelled "Unfreeze!" and stomped into the next passenger car.

A small whimper came from the back of the train car. Heads swung. Amethyst could not believe her eyes.

Emmy and Rachel were snuggled tightly in a back seat.

Amethyst rushed to them. "What are you doing here? Did you hide?"

Emmy shook her small head. "No. The meanie put us here. She say, 'No move.' So we not move."

"You can move now," said Emily softly. "I promise."

Emmy carefully got up, holding Rachel's hand very tightly. Mary saw them and smiled. "Are you okay, girls? What are your names?"

"Emmy," whispered Emmy, "and this is my sissy, Rachel."

"Is Emmy short for Emily?" Emily wanted to know.

"No," said Emmy, puzzled. "I fink.... I fink... I not remember what it short for."

"But it is short for something?" asked Amethyst.

"Yea," said Rachel. "My name short for something too."

"What?" asked McKenna.

"I fink Rachella?" said Rachel.

"That's a nice name," said Courtney. "Can I call you Rachella?"

"No," said Rachel. "Rachel my name. I not want to be called Rachella. That's not a petty name."

"That's fine, darling," said Mary. Then she turned to them all.

She opened her mouth to say something, then stopped. Then she said, "I need your help, Amethyst. I gave you help, now you need to give me help."

"Yes, what is it?" Amethyst climbed on top of a seat and fiddled with the window. Locked. She moved onto the next one.

"Well, it's a long story," started Mary. "I can't tell you all of it now."

"You can tell me," pried Amethyst, meddling with a third window.

"We.... need..." Mary chose her words carefully. "We need.... to find something."

"Like hide-and-seek?" Emmy lit up. "Oh, I love hide-and-seek!"

"So do I!" Rachel and Lucy said in unison.

"Almost," said Mary.

"What is it we need to find?" Amethyst was so excited she accidentally missed the fourth window and went on to a fifth.

Josh noticed and silently tried to unlock the fourth.

"A ring," said Mary, "a magic ring. It can rotate its shape, too."

"Then you should call it a magical shape-shifter," McKenna suggested.

"Good idea, whatever-your-name-is," said Mary, "but if this makes any sense at all, it's not a magical shape-shifter. It's a ring that can shape-shift."

"Got it." Amethyst moved on to a sixth window. "Is it yours, Mary?"

"No, not exactly, but I need to have it."

"You want me to steal it?" Amethyst stopped trying to find a lock on the window and looked over at Mary. Maybe Mary wasn't the trustworthy person she thought she was after all!

"No, no." Mary looked as if she was searching for words. "It's... it's.. Oh, I don't know how to explain it."

Amethyst just kept staring at Mary. She moved onto the seventh window slowly, staring at Mary the whole time.

"By the way," McKenna said, "my name is *not* 'whatever-your-name-is'. It's McKenna."

But everyone ignored her.

Mary said, "It's hidden somewhere in this world and we need to find it before somebody else does."

"Eugenia?" guessed Amethyst.

"I can't say who yet."

Mary frowned. "Will you help me?" She looked over at Amethyst, who was now on the opposite side of the train, trying to open the eighth window.

"Yes," said Amethyst slowly.

Over the next few hours, Amethyst tried every single thing she thought of to get the windows open, so they might escape. After a while Emily and Josh joined in. Then Courtney, McKenna, and Angelica.

But every window was securely locked and no one could find the lock anywhere. After they'd been trying for an hour and a half, Josh slumped over in a seat. "There's only one more thing to try- breaking the window." But the window was as tough as tough could get. Nothing they tried could break it.

Finally they gave up and started to sing. Amethyst had suggested it. "I feel like annoying Eugenia," she had said. Therefore they had spent a half hour singing loud, obnoxious songs. But Eugenia never came in to say "be quiet". They didn't even hear any sounds of frustration. But they kept on singing anyway.

Around six o'clock, Eugenia entered the train car with plates of bread and beans and water. The water was cleaner now, the beans were not as soggy, and the bread had butter.

When she had handed out everything, Eugenia pointed to Amethyst, who was taking a bite of bread. "You," she snapped, "come here."

Amethyst swallowed her bite whole and got up obediently.

"Snap your fingers," commanded Eugenia, pointing a bony finger at Amethyst.

Amethyst hesitated.

"If you don't, there will be serious consequences," warned Eugenia.

Amethyst snapped— and blinked in confusion. Impossible! She couldn't have seen sparks fly out from her fingers! She snapped again. Yes, she had. Every time she snapped, sparks flew out from her fingers, then dissolved. She grinned. Maybe she could figure out how to do a firework show by snapping! Now, that would be a fine way to spend her time! Wait until she told Josh her idea! He'd love it! She was about to go over to him, but then Eugenia commanded that she had to jump.

Amethyst didn't hesitate this time. She just went right ahead and jumped. She had never tried before because the asylum's rules had been no jumping, and she was surprised how high she could jump. And she landed so gracefully. She laughed aloud and spent five minutes jumping up and down, until Eugenia yelled "Quit it, brat!" Then she commanded:

"Walk to the other side of this train car and back."

Amethyst did, but her mind was not really on her walking, but on her jumping. Then she had a great idea— she and Josh could put on a play! She grinned at the idea.

"Feel light on your feet, bratty child?" cackled Eugenia, startling her thoughts.

Amethyst thought. Yes, she did feel light. Very light. She giggled. What more could she do? Fly? But then she was struck by a troubling thought: why did Eugenia have her do things that were fun?

"Go back and eat," said Eugenia. Amethyst did, confused of why Eugenia had wanted to know. She watched Eugenia as she exited the car.

Amethyst hurriedly ate up her beans. "It's so cool," she said to Josh. "And I was thinking— me and you could put on a firework show! And a jumping show! Isn't that a fab idea?"

Josh nodded, his eyes full of envy.

Just then Eugenia came back in to collect plates. She looked at them all and gave them a wicked smile.

Then she grabbed Lucy roughly and told her to do the same

things she had Amethyst do. Amethyst noticed the results of Lucy were the same as hers. *That's peculiar*, she thought.

Then Eugenia had Angelica and the others do the same.

Every girl's (and Josh's) results were the same. They all felt light on their feet; they all could jump high; they all had something.... sparks, was it?... come out of their fingers when they snapped. It was confusing for Amethyst. Could everyone do that, or just her and the others?

Amethyst watched them in confusion. Lucy seemed frightened, like Angelica and McKenna; while Courtney and Emily giggled softly; and Josh was simply screaming in delight that he could do the stuff too.

After Eugenia left, Josh nudged her. "Why'd the fairy do that?" he asked her. "I mean, I'm glad she did, because I love being able to do this stuff- but why?"

Amethyst shrugged. "I don't know any more than you do." Josh shrugged, too, and snapped his fingers. A spark flew out. "Firework!" he cried. "Hey, let's do that firework show now - let's just hope the car doesn't catch on fire!"

Amethyst looked on politely, but her mind was on something else.... something Angelica had told her way back in the boxcar.... what was it? She frowned. Aha! That was it! Angelica had said, 'Well, she can get a flame on a candle just by snapping her fingers.' and 'she can make fireworks by snapping her fingers.' In other words, Eugenia had sparks fly from her fingers when she snapped.... just like Amethyst, Josh, and the others! What was the connection? She thought about it long and hard. Amethyst certainly wasn't a fairy, but maybe she was under a wish that made her be able to do it? Or maybe all human beings could? Amethyst had never been in public places besides the asylum so she didn't know.

Amethyst was troubled about this and had a hard time getting to sleep. Things were getting more and more confusing. When she drifted off, the words "She can get a flame on a candle just by snapping her fingers," echoed over and over in her mind. *She can get a flame on a candle just by snapping her fingers..... just by snapping her fingers.. just by snapping her fingers.*

chapter nine
Queen Mahalia's Castle

In the morning, Amethyst felt better.

She felt more confident about Eugenia and that she could figure out what she was up to. But she decided she'd put it off until later.

The rest of the day she made the best of it. During lunch, which was a spoonful of refried beans (which Amethyst enjoyed much more than the other ones), a piece of wheat bread with butter, and water, she made up jokes about Eugenia and the train. In the afternoon, she and Josh put together a firework show (secretly in hopes of burning the door off) and she and Angelica (with help from McKenna, Courtney, Lucy, Rachel, Emmy and Emily) put on a play.

After they were done, they flopped down, exhausted, onto a train seat, sweating but happy.

"You know," said Amethyst, wiping her forehead with her

hand, "it actually isn't that bad, on the train. I mean, there's lots of things we can do, and we haven't even ventured out into the other cars yet!"

Mary looked at her quickly. "As long as Eugenia is on the train, I'm not having you going out of this car."

Josh let out a sigh. "That's okay," he said finally.

Suddenly, in her quiet little voice, Lucy said, "Amethyst, I'm worried. Worried about where this train is going."

"We too," chorused Emmy and Rachel.

"I am too, girls," said Amethyst sadly. "But we've tried everything. There's nothing left we can do to get out."

"I know," said Lucy. "Mary?"

"Yes, dear?" said Mary.

"Do you know where this train is going?"

"No, I don't, darling." Mary frowned. "You'd better not ask Eugenia, either. She'll just get mad."

Lucy nodded. "I'll never say anything."

"Us neither," said Rachel and Emmy.

"Good," said Mary. She leaned back in her seat. "Now, I've been looking forward to tonight's play. Do you know when it starts....."

"It starts now!" announced Rachel.

And that was how they spent the rest of their evening: performing plays for Mary. And though they knew that any day they would arrive where Eugenia wanted them, they were able to enjoy their evening in the train car on the dreaded orphan train.

After a couple days, the train skidded to a halt. Amethyst was half glad and half not. The ride had been long, despite the fact she and Josh had put together the best firework shows, and she had memorized the car inch by inch. But she didn't want to go anywhere Eugenia wanted her to go, because who knew how bad it'd be?

Then into the car came Eugenia, wearing the brightest yellow suit you could imagine. The sun reflected off it, too, making it seem even more yellow.

Eugenia instructed them to take hands or serious consequences would occur. Amethyst doubted there was any consequence, but she did what Eugenia said anyway, because she didn't want to risk it, and she certainly didn't want to get tied up.

Eugenia instructed them to follow her then, and they did.

They followed her past coffee shops, clothing stores, grocery stores, until finally they came to a big field. Way off in the distance a tiny castle shone. *It must be humungous up close*, thought Amethyst.

"There," snarled Eugenia, pointing to the castle with a yellow-gloved finger, "is our destination."

"No," said Mary. "You're not getting us in there."

"Why not?" asked Amethyst. The castle was gorgeous, even from far off! *Why would Mary not want us to go in there?* she wondered.

"Good question, ugly one," said Eugenia, smiling wickedly. "Why not? It doesn't matter what your reason is, anyway, because we are going in there!" She started off again, and everyone followed slowly, even Mary.

After a couple of hours of saying jokes then being hushed by Eugenia, they reached the castle and all of them followed Eugenia up the steps.

But when Eugenia grasped the brass doorknob, Mary said, "Stop!" She stormed out of line, but then returned at Eugenia's fierce look.

"No way," laughed Eugenia and opened the doors. "Let's see some magic from you, then."

Mary can't do magic! Amethyst wanted to shout, but she stayed quiet.

"I will, if you do any on any of these children," Mary said back.

Eugenia narrowed her eyes. "Fine, then. Have it your way. Let's see something from you." She waved her hand and closed her eyes, then snapped her fingers ten times in a row, pointing her finger at Lucy the whole time.

A parade of sparks rose from her fingers, and surrounded Lucy. Lucy rose. She rose up, up, then came down in front of Eugenia, who grabbed her by her hair. Lucy screamed.

"Stop!" commanded Mary. Amethyst felt bad for Mary.

Mary was acting like the President. The only president she could be was the President of Orphan Asylums. And she probably was not. Besides, against Eugenia, Mary was powerless.

Eugenia cackled and held Lucy tighter. "Freeze," she said, touching Lucy. "Mouth too," she corrected, when Lucy opened her mouth.

"You've gone too far!" said Mary, outraged.

"Well, do some magic!" said the evil fairy, leading them all into the castle, still dragging Lucy by the hair.

Amethyst, Angelica, Josh and all the others exchanged worried glances as they were forced into the grand castle, with glistening walls and beautiful decor. Angelica said "Ooh," instantly. Amethyst opened her mouth to say it too, but Mary silenced her with a fierce look.

Eugenia led them past doors, doors, and more doors, and down a long hallway. They took turns, curved, and past more doors. They went up stairs, stairs, and more stairs, then they went down stairs, and curved, curved, and turned..... Amethyst was getting tired. Her feet ached. Her legs ached. And she ached from being captive, if there was a way to do so.

Finally, Eugenia came to the end of a hallway. *Now I'll have to take several more turns*, though Amethyst angrily.

But instead, Eugenia stopped at a shiny door decorated in rubies, sapphires, pearls, and- Amethyst grinned- amethysts. The jewels sent off glistening lights through the hallway. Amethyst wondered how somebody so evil could have a castle so pretty.

Eugenia then turned around and looked at her captives.

"You'd better behave yourself here," she warned. It was a hint of a wish, but it had no effect; Eugenia had not used her wand.

Mary stormed out of the line and up to Eugenia. "We're not going in there. Try all you like, we're not." She stood face-to-face with Eugenia, and Amethyst thought she saw a quick flicker of fright in the fairy's eyes. Mary's eyes, however, were blazing. She was very, very mad. After a while, when Eugenia said nothing, Mary repeated, "We're. Not. Going. In. That. Room. No. Matter. What. You. Say."

"How do you know what's in there?" asked McKenna rudely.

"I just do," replied Mary, never taking her eyes off Eugenia. "Let Lucy go, and lead us out of this place. I will use you-know-what if you do not."

Amethyst wondered if you-know-what was magic. Could Mary really do magic? She reconsidered. Of course not. Mary was just an ordinary human being, right?

"Should I use you-know-what to make you not do you-know-what?" asked Eugenia in a teasing tone. "And no, I shall not release Lulu, nor lead you away. Mahalia is counting on me, and I have been waiting for this moment for years, anyway." Her eyes blazed, then, too, only hers blazed not in anger, but in wickedness. Then she leaned in and whispered something to Mary. Mary's face grew pale.

Eugenia led the way into the glamorous room. Amethyst and her friends hesitated at first, but then Eugenia threateningly pulled out her wand and made to wave it, so all of them, even Mary, stumbled into the room.

It was huge; with blooming flowers and gems everywhere, and pictures of beautiful fairies on the walls, and stained-glass windows. In the back of the grand room there was a shiny red velvet throne. The armrests were brass, and jewels decorated it.

But when Amethyst saw the person that sat on the throne, she nearly fainted in horror. The person looked exactly like Amethyst's vision of how the most evil person on earth would look like.

The person had a long blue dress, decorated in dirty sapphires, and pitch black hair braided around her body. Her earrings, huge grimy sapphires, dangled at least two feet past her ears. Her lipstick was black and her lips were puffy and big. Her sharp fingers curled around an elegant, long wand with a ruby tip. When she smiled, she displayed black teeth as black as her hair. Her crown was at least three feet high and covered with grimy jewels and broken glass, as if someone had pounded rocks on it for hours on end. But what made Amethyst almost fall over was her eyes. They were bright red. Every bit of it. There seemed to be no white-part or pupil, only red, red, red.

The person smiled, showing her black teeth, and said, "Ah, Eugenia, you managed to do it at last. I am everlastingly proud."

Her voice was also villainous, decided Amethyst. It was a mix between a croak, a neigh, a quack and a squeak. It sounded almost as bad as the orphan train's squeaky whistle.

"Aye, I did, Queen Mahalia," said Eugenia proudly.

Queen Mahalia got down from her throne, and walked past Amethyst and all the others until she got to Mary. She looked in her eyes and narrowed her own. "Did you finally surrender, Mary? I think you might've. After all, why else would Mahalia- me- have you?" She grinned evilly.

Mary shook her head stubbornly. "I didn't surrender to you; I never intend to. I simply was captured by your ugly accomplice."

Queen Mahalia rolled her eyes, smiled an evil smile and went up to Eugenia, who had Lucy. "This is the gal?" she asked with a hint of disgust, looking the little horrified girl up and down.

"Yes, your Highness," said Eugenia obediently. "She was easy to get, too. She barely fought, unlike the rest."

"She's lying!" Emmy screamed. "*I* fought better than Lucy! I was the strongest!"

"No, *I* was the strongest!" whined Rachel. "Miss Queen, tell her *I* was the best!"

"You aren't the best," said Mahalia. "You were both horrible." The two girls screeched.

"Now, back to the gal..." Lucy's eyes were wide with fear.

Amethyst worried for her friend and gripped Josh's hand even harder. How much could this.... this.... fairy do to them?

Mahalia waved her wand in the air, creating a blaze of sparks. "All these years," she said, "and we've finally captured the queen."

What in the world? Lucy is not a queen! thought Amethyst, then reconsidered. *Or was she?*

chapter ten
Shrieking, a Plan, and a Little Mixed-Up Wish

And," Mahalia went on, "we finally captured the others, too. The all-evil-no-good quest has succeeded. It was such a good idea to ask Odelia and Quiana to help out, too, Eugenia."

"Thank you," said Eugenia in a voice that was as humble as a villain's voice could get. Amethyst shivered.

Mahalia took Lucy from Eugenia. "Poor little thing," she said, looking down at Lucy. "Too bad we must rid ourselves of her."

"We could keep her," suggested Eugenia, "and make her a slave."

Mahalia shook her head and raised her wand. "I wish" - Mary was too fast. Realizing Mahalia's plot, Mary dashed toward her, and in one swift move snatched the wand away. Then she raised the wand herself and made a wish-

"I wish Mahalia would set all nine of us free!"

Mahalia looked startled, then her mouth started to move and she started to talk, but it was magic making the words, not her. "Go, captives, leave at once. Nine of you may go." From magic, she raised her arms in the air.

"We're freeeee!" yelled McKenna joyfully.

"Yippee!" Courtney joined in the cheering and bumped up against the door.

"We're freeeeeeeeeeeee!" yelled McKenna again, beginning to spin towards the door. But she had forgotten Courtney was there, and she spun right into the dazed girl.

"McKENNA!" Courtney practically screamed. "We're freed, and the first thing you do is collide into me? You must be still adjusting to not being frozen!"

"Sorrrrrry!" yelled McKenna, spinning in the other direction and this time colliding into Mahalia and knocking her crown off.

"Sorry!" She lay on the floor for a minute, then got up and began to spin again, until Courtney grabbed her shoulders. "Stop it, we've got to get out of here before the magic wears off!"

"Okaaaaaaay!" yelled McKenna.

"And enough with the shrieking!" Courtney replied desperately.

They all rushed towards the doors, McKenna still ignoring Courtney and yelling, "We're freeeeeeeee!" and waving her arms in the air.

"Hey," said Mahalia. "One of you has to stay here. I have the rights. You have ten. Only nine people I let go."

Mary's mouth went dry as she did the math.

"How nice of you to let me pick," said Mahalia although Mary had done no such thing. "I pick..." She grabbed Lucy.

"Lulu!"

"She's Lucy," said Emmy. "You do know name-calling is hurtful?"

"Yes it is, Ello," said Mahalia teasingly.

"My name is Emmy," said Emmy. She was getting mad. "That's to you, Calia-balia!"

"Calia-balia, calia-balia," sang Rachel.

"Shut your mouth, ugly ones!" said Eugenia.

Mary walked over and pulled out the wand she had snatched from Mahalia.

"If you do that," Mahalia said, "you and your friends will suffer, because I will use Eugenia's wand."

Mary narrowed her eyes, trying to ignore Mahalia's threats. "Let her go."

"No way," said Eugenia. "We're not dummies."

"Yes you are," insisted McKenna. "You're *really* dumb dummies."

Mahalia ignored her, although it was clear she heard.

"Why don't you do as you wished, Mary? Leave this castle! Go away free!"

"I will,"said Mary, "but I'll be back." She crouched down to look at Lucy. "I have a job for you," she said. "A top-secret agent job." She whispered in the little girl's ear, "I want you to drive Mahalia so crazy she lets you go. And while you're doing that you need to spy."

Lucy smiled a little, but the fear in her eyes remained. She seemed to be saying, "I can't believe you're doing this to me."

Amethyst couldn't believe it either. She held onto Josh.

Mary slowly led them out. "We'll be back, Lucy, and remember your mission." They sadly left the castle and made their way to a little park. It was quiet, with nobody to eavesdrop or disturb them.

Mary looked around, found a shady tree to sit under, and said, "I need to talk to you guys. Big stuff."

"Yea?" Amethyst seated herself between Emmy, Rachel, and Mary.

"I know you.... don't see the importance of the ring I talked about on the train," said Mary.

"No," admitted Amethyst.

"Well.... the ring can free people and set them free."

"Lucy!" cried Josh.

"Yes...." Mary looked disappointed. "Amethyst, is there any other person who needs to be set free?"

Amethyst thought. "Yes! My mother. Well, maybe not set free." She blinked back tears. "Just.... I don't know where she is." Amethyst saw something.... hope, was it?.. in Mary's eyes. "Do you know where she is?"

"Well......yes, in a way, I do."

"Where is she?" Amethyst was filled up with hope.

Mary hesitated. "I can't tell you right now, honey cake."

There was that expression again! Where had she heard it before?

"*Please?*"

"No. Amethyst honey cake.... did you know you have sisters?"

"I do?" Amethyst was puzzled. "I don't remember having them. And how do you know?"

Mary smiled. "I am a good friend of your mother's. Trust me. You have four sisters."

"Where are they? Who are they?"

"I'm not sure if you know the third one," said Mary hesitantly. "And I'm going to let you figure out who the fourth one is."

"Please, tell me." If she couldn't have her mother, could she have her sisters, whoever they were?

"Their names are Sapphire, Emerald, Topaz, and Opal."

Amethyst sighed happily. So her mother had named her children after jewels. She hoped Mary knew where her sisters were. She could not contain her excitement.

"Such pretty names." She was sad, however, that they weren't somebody she knew.

"What's wrong, honey cake?" Mary's voice was worried.

"Nothing, Mary.... it's just that I was hoping I knew my sisters already."

"Their names were changed," said Mary. "When they were taken to an asylum the managers changed their names."

Emily, shyly, looked up. "Am I a sister of her? I vaguely remember being called Opal before I was thrown on the orphan train."

"No, you don't look like Amethyst's mother, and I saw them when they came to the same asylum, except for the fourth, who went to.... live elsewhere. Sorry, dear." She saw Emily's sad face. "But you may have used to be called Opal, still."

"Tell me, Mary." Amethyst's voice was begging.

"Two of them are here right now. They're twins."

Amethyst sucked in her breath so fast she nearly fell over.

Her eyes scavenged her friends until she found the two four-year-olds she was looking for. "All this time?" she said. "All this time and.... Emmy and Rachel were my sisters?"

"Big sissy!" cried Rachel and Emmy, throwing their arms around her legs.

"Did you know?" Amethyst asked suspiciously, hugging them back.

"They didn't," said Mary.

"This is quite a reunion," commented McKenna. "So, let me guess. Rachel is Emerald and Emmy is Sapphire."

"No," said Mary. "Rachel is Sapphire and Emmy is Topaz."

Amethyst had a question she wanted to ask, but she was afraid to ask it. "Where's.... where's my other sister?" She knew Mary for some reason wanted to keep the fourth one secret, so she pretended she only had three. She desperately wanted to know the fourth; but so far Mary had proven trustworthy and so Amethyst trusted her. And if Mary said they'd keep the fourth sister a secret, that's what they'd do.

"She's your twin, but you aren't identical."

"And she was at my asylum?"

"I believe so."

"I'm bored," complained McKenna. "Can we go play Race, Courtney?"

"No, McKenna, leave me alone."

"I'll play, McKenna." Angelica stood up. "Tell me when

you're done talking. No offense, Mary, it's kind of boring for me."

"I'll play, too, if you don't mind," said Emily shyly.

"Go right ahead," said Mary. "Do you guys want to play, Emmy and Rachel?"

"We want to be with Big Sissy," they said.

"Okay. Courtney, you sure you don't want to play?" Mary asked.

"Well.... okay." Courtney stood up. "But I'm only playing because I want to, not because McKenna asked me to, okay?"

"Okay." Mary smiled.

"I'll stay, thank you," said Josh.

Mary cuddled Amethyst and began again. "Well, your sister's 'new' name is Miranda."

Amethyst jumped right up. "NO WAY! She was my friend at that awful place! We need to get back there, Mary!"

Mary sighed. "We can't. We have to find the magic ring first."

Amethyst's excitement faded away. "But, Mary-"

"The magic ring will rescue Miranda," said Mary, "or Emerald, her given name. Plus it will destroy all evil."

"Like, perhaps, Miss Quiana?" asked Josh. "Is she evil enough to be considered evil?"

Mary thought. "I think so."

"Is Miss Odelia on the evil list? At my asylum she was nasty."

"If she was nasty she's on the list. Now, my honey cake, call in the girls, will you? I have to explain the ring."

They stood hesitantly, not sure to whom Mary was talking to.

"Amethyst, please do as I ask."

Amethyst, relieved Mary had been talking to her, went into the playing area. "McKenna, Courtney, Emily, Angelica," she called, "Mary wants you guys."

They obediently followed Amethyst back to Mary.

"Guys and girls," said Mary, "do you want to help rescue Amethyst's long-lost sister, by finding a magic ring, or would you like to go back to living at your asylums?"

They all agreed they'd rather help. "Alright...now don't worry, Amethyst, this will turn out fine," Mary added, seeing Amethyst's doubtful look.

"Can't we just, like, rescue Miranda and then find the ring?" asked Amethyst.

"Do you seriously think Miss Odelia will just give Miranda to me?"

"No," admitted Amethyst uncomfortably.

"Well, then. We'll find this ring."

"Why does it need finding?" asked McKenna.

"Well, a long time ago, I owned this ring. But somebody evil- I will not say who- took it. But one of my associates spotted the villain, snatched the ring from her, and hid it. Unfortunately, she died before she revealed its whereabouts. But I do know she changed the activation process in order to keep the evil fairies from activating and using the ring for evil purposes."

Amethyst frowned and said, "So the ring is somewhere in this world, but no one knows where."

"Correct," said Mary.

"Do we have any leads to where it'd be? Any clues?" questioned Courtney.

"If we knew that, Courtney," said McKenna, "it wouldn't be lost."

"Now, girls. We just need to figure out what city we should start looking in," said Mary.

"Maybe it's in Las Vegas," urged Josh.

"Bangladesh!" declared McKenna. ("That's a country, McKenna, not a city!")

Mary shook her head. "I don't know where the ring is, but I do have pretty good instinct." Mary shrugged. "I have a good feeling about Rome."

"Why Rome?" asked Amethyst.

"The last thing I remember my associate saying was something about Rome."

Courtney wasn't listening, meanwhile. She was staring at Mary in a daze. She loved any kind of gem, and was terrifically happy; their quest was going to be searching for a gem, while surrounded by gems! Ah, the wonderful, glorious joy of gems!

"Courtney, quit daydreaming!" accused Angelica. "I know your obsession for rocks, but this is no time to daydream! We've got work to do!"

Courtney snapped out of her daze. "I am *not* obsessed with rocks."

Mary nodded absentmindedly. "We've got to go. We'll start out in Rome, like I said."

They all nodded in agreement. Emily was already thinking of what awesome stuff they would be able to do with a magic ring. Put an end to all evildoers? Make herself and the others live forever? Give us our own castle?

As if reading her thoughts, Mary said, "We can't keep it for ourselves, of course. After we rescue Miranda, we'll have to return the ring to its case beneath the sea."

"Why beneath the sea?" asked McKenna. "Why not somewhere else?"

Mary told her slowly evil fairies could not survive in water, and the whole time McKenna stared at her like she was not understanding, but at the end she nodded just like an adult.

"But don't we need to rid ourselves of those dirty little pests?" Josh asked, making up a new name to call the evil fairies.

"The dirty little pests, eh?" Mary asked, laughing. "Yes, we do! Thank you for reminding me, young man! Don't forget, kids, we also need to rescue Lucy."

Amethyst was confused. "How'll we know it's the ring when we find it?"

"Because it'll 'sparkle like a star and shine like a jewel,' " said Mary, obviously quoting, although Amethyst had no idea what she was quoting from.

"So, when we find it, if we find it, we're first rescuing Miranda and Lucy, then we're destroying all of the dirty little pests. Then-"

McKenna interrupted. She chanted, "The dirty little pests! The dirty little pests! The-"

"Could I continue?" asked Amethyst rudely. "And then we

will be returning the ring to its case beneath the sea, and almost the whole time being chased by the dirty little pests..." She paused, waiting for the interruption she was sure was coming.

It did. McKenna said once again, "The dirty little pests! The dirty little pests! The dirrrrrrttty littttttttle peeessssstttsss!" She droned out on the last notes, her mouth wide open.

Then she noticed someone else was talking. She shut her mouth, looking at Amethyst. "Oopsie-doopsie. Sorry, go ahead, Ammmmmethyst!"

Amethyst rolled her eyes, but finished, "...while being chased by you-know-who, and when we're done we can retire."

Mary nodded.

And everyone saw just how risky the plan was.

chapter eleven
A Little Bit of Airplane Trouble

The next morning, after a night in the park, Mary woke the children with a start. "Wake up, boys and girls! Our flight is leaving soon!"

"Flight?" mumbled Amethyst, half-awake. "We can't fly....."

"Silly girl, we're not flying. We're riding a plane," said Mary matter-of-factly. "Open your eyes, kids. Let's get a-" She stopped mid-sentence. What she was going to say was 'let's get a move-on,' but then she was sure McKenna would interrupt with her chants, and she wasn't in the mood to deal with chanting. So she stopped.

"Plane?" Amethyst woke up all the way, sat up, and rubbed her eyes. "Yeah... when are we leaving?"

"In ten minutes. Our flight's at one o'clock, and it's already eight o' clock, and besides, we'll have to walk."

"Can we eat breakfast first?" mumbled Josh. "I'm hungry."

"*Breakfast!*" Mary flew into a panic. "Oh yeah- you guys haven't eaten in a while! I completely forgot! I'm *so* sorry. Well, I guess we have time to eat, but only if we get up NOW!"

Josh stood up, stretched and yawned. "That's good with me. Can we have pancakes?"

"No," said Mary briskly. "We'll stop at a coffee shop for donuts once we reach town."

Donuts. Amethyst got up at the word. She had never eaten a donut and was very eager to try one. Once everyone was up and they reached town, Mary looked around for a coffee shop. She found one quickly and they entered.

Mary pulled out her wallet. She ordered a bag of donut holes - some type of donut Amethyst had never heard of - and sat them down at a table. She passed them out, two for each person. "Make it last," she said. "We may not get to eat until we land."

"I just hope Lucy is getting sweets, too," said Angelica quietly, and everyone nodded in agreement.

Amethyst felt like punching Mahalia and Eugenia and all the other evil fairies. She couldn't help hissing, "Wait until I get my hands on her...." The whole table erupted in laughter. Amethyst felt her cheeks reddening in embarrassment. She picked up a donut hole and bit in. It was powdery and soft and sugary. *Bliss!*

She had just finished eating the delicious donut when Mary announced it was time to go. "We can have more to eat when we reach Rome," she promised. Amethyst hurriedly popped the other donut hole in her mouth. They all exited the shop and made their way to the airport. Everyone was excited.

Amethyst gazed up at the big plane and hoped she didn't get sick or scared. She felt excitement all over, as she had never been in a plane before.

Since they had come from a orphan-train they of course had no bags so they headed straight for the plane. They made their way through security with no issues at all. It was so quick and easy, in fact, that Mary began to wonder if it was too easy. The kids seemed oblivious and began to sing as they boarded the plane.

Amethyst was surprised at how close the seats were together as McKenna and Courtney fought over the window seat.

Mary sat down and breathed a deep breath as the plane rose in the air. Behind her, Amethyst looked out her window and spotted a familiar place. "Look, it's Queen Mahalia's castle!" Then she closed her eyes, not wanting to see it, and instructed Angelica to tell her when they passed it. When she opened her eyes again she found they were high above the ground. Everything was small and tiny and Amethyst was awed. "I hope Mahalia's castle doesn't come by again," she said to herself.

"Yes, Mahalia's castle," mused a familiar voice from behind her. Amethyst swung around, startled. She saw a woman with spiky hair and red lips. She had piercing green eyes and was holding a little black purse. Her fingernails were painted a hideous orange, the type of orange you only had to look at to feel ill.

"Yes, the queen's castle," repeated the lady. Amethyst knew she'd seen this lady before, but where? She was so hidden beneath makeup she couldn't tell.

"I think we should go there, why not?" said the lady wickedly. She reached into her purse and pulled out a slim stick. A *wand!*

"Uh.... Mary?" Amethyst said uneasily, edging away from the weird lady. She glanced out the window. How long had they been on the plane? Ten minutes?

"Good choice," said the lady, even though Amethyst hadn't made a choice. The lady looked deep into Amethyst as she stood up. Without turning her head, she reached up with one hand and pulled a lever on her window, and with her other hand dislodged it.

Suddenly, Amethyst couldn't breathe as the plane went into chaos. Everyone was screaming but the lady took no notice.

"Mary!" Amethyst tried to scream. Her eyes wide, her hands clenching the leather seat as her feet lifted off the floor.

Her stomach dropped as the plane changed altitude quickly. She screamed again as an oxygen mask smacked her in the face.

Amethyst watched in horror as the lady swiftly pried her friends' fingers loose. One by one they were sucked out of the rapidly descending plane.

The lady then turned and saw Amethyst and Angelica still on the plane, staring at the hole through which the others had fallen.

She grabbed the screaming Angelica, hurling her through the air into the hole. Angelica screeched and grabbed hold on the edge, but just barely. The lady, however, ignored her and went for Amethyst. Amethyst saw it coming and gripped the seat even tighter, screaming with all her strength. The lady came towards her and in one quick motion grabbed her wrists. Amethyst screamed again, but it was no use. The lady swung her over the edge of the opening. Amethyst tumbled down, screaming and yelling, and at the last second managed to grab onto Angelica's ankle. Angelica groaned, and her grip began to loosen. The lady saw, and came over. Giving Amethyst and Angelica a wicked grin, she reached down and grabbed Angelica's hands right off the plane side, and held them in the air for a moment before simply letting go. Angelica and Amethyst screamed, plummeting down, down, down.

Before the plane was completely out of sight, Amethyst looked up and saw the lady pull out a parasol, open it and jump from the plane.

Amethyst's life flashed before her eyes. Arriving at the asylum, going on the orphan train, meeting Mary, the long train ride, Mahalia's castle.... Her mother.... Her mother. Who was her mother? Now she would probably never find out. Her friends.... were they alright? As she fell, a strange sensation came over her. She felt peaceful, calm, as if.... *as if she had been here before.*

Then the world went black.

chapter twelve
Castle Again?

The hard, cold floor beneath Amethyst woke her up. She couldn't believe her eyes as she sat up and looked around. Josh, Courtney, McKenna, Angelica, Emily, Rachel, and Emmy were all lying face-down on the floor. *What...?* thought Amethyst, blinking. *Where am I? How did I get here?*

"You okay, Amethyst honey cake?" A familiar voice startled Amethyst's thoughts. She looked around. Mary was sitting in front of her. She looked worried.

"Yep," said Amethyst, rubbing her eyes, "but where are we?"

Mary said glumly, "Mahalia's castle."

"Oh *no*," said Amethyst.

Angelica peeled her face off the floor. "Ugh-ugh-ugh. So, we're in Queen whatever-her-name-is's castle, right?" She rubbed her face vigorously. "My nose hurts."

"Mine too," mumbled Josh, his face still on the floor.

Mary sighed, walked over to him, and pulled him up.

"Ow!" he cried. "Why'd you do that?"

Mary grinned. "You can't stay like that forever."

"Can I?" asked McKenna. "My eyebrow hurts."

"Get up, silly girl," said Mary, "and get Courtney up while you're at it. I'll get up Emily, and Amethyst, you take care of the twins."

McKenna got up. She grinned. "Thanks a ton, Mary. I have a perfect idea on how to get Courtney up." She went over to Courtney and yelled in her ear, "WAKE UP, SLEEPYHEAD!"

"Hey," yelped Courtney, sitting up. "Geez, McKenna, did you *have* to do *that?*"

"Yes," said McKenna honestly. "You should be thanking me. I got you up without pulling your face *or* your hair! I didn't even touch you!"

"Girls, girls, stop quarreling," said Angelica.

"We're not quarreling," they said in unison.

"Jinx, you owe me a soda." McKenna sounded pleased.

"Huh?" asked Courtney. She raised her eyebrows.

"Nothing. Just remember I need two dollars from you to buy a soda when we get back to the city."

"Whatever," said Courtney. "I don't even *have* two dollars."

Suddenly, Mahalia's voice came. "Where are my new captives Miss Odelia promised me? Oh, here they are. Where's Odelia, girlies and boysies?"

" 'Boysies' isn't a word," said Josh, annoyed.

"Why do I care?" bellowed Mahalia. "I'll repeat myself-where's Odelia, you fools?"

"I don't know!" yelled Amethyst, "maybe she died."

"Did you...." Mahalia narrowed her eyes. "Oh, why do I care? Follow me, fools. I'll take care of you myself."

"Wait! Here I am!" There was a burst of sparks and Miss Odelia stood there. Amethyst immediately recognized her as the lady from the plane. "They threw me off course."

"Did not," said McKenna. "We were all falling. You simply fell the wrong way."

"You can't fall the wrong way, fool," said Mahalia.

"You can if you make yourself purposely do it," protested

Angelica. "Besides, it wasn't our fault. If you'd kept us on the plane, you'd never would've been thrown off track."

"Ha!" said Miss Odelia. "I think not! You're aware the pilot was none other than Miss Quiana, right?"

Emily shook her head. "No way." She spoke for all of them but Mary. Mary was thinking, *So that's why I heard cackling.*

"Yes way," said Mahalia. "Come on, you fools."

"I did make a wish," said Mary. "You can't recapture us. You won't be able to."

"Says who?" asked Mahalia mockingly. "The queen? Oh, she can't- I'm the queen around here! And you know: I made a wish, too. I used Eugenia's spare wand. I wished your wish would not work and that I would be able to capture you. That was before I walked in and saw your gross little faces."

Miss Odelia cocked her head. "Eugenia says they're ugly."

"Ugly, gross, whatever-you-are," said Mahalia, "come with me." They reluctantly followed, Mahalia in the lead, Odelia at the back.

They went through so many hallways and past so many doors Amethyst thought she'd get sick. Finally they stopped in a narrow room. It was painted a dull brown and had no windows.

Mahalia grinned evilly as she pushed them into the room. "We can't have little girls out looking for a magic ring, now can we?" she cackled, and slammed the door shut. Amethyst thought she heard a key click in the lock.

Trembling, Emily asked, "Mary.... will we be alright?"

"Of course not," teased Mahalia from the outside. Startled, everyone grew quiet, and it was a good thing they did, because otherwise they would not have been able to hear what Mahalia whispered to Miss Odelia.

chapter thirteen
Rome Street!

"We've got a head start, at least, Odelia," she whispered. "The kids are locked up, and I just found out the ring is located on Rome Street."

"Fantastic," said Miss Odelia, and then Amethyst heard their footsteps fade away.

"Rome Street!" exclaimed Mary. "Rome Street - that was it! Not Rome itself! We've *got* to find a map!"

McKenna got up and walked to the door. She turned the handle, expecting it to be locked. But instead.... it opened! "Hey!" she cried in a singsong voice, "I found *another* way they're dummies!"

All eyes went to her, and the open door. "How...." began Amethyst but McKenna cut her off.

"They left it unlocked. See? They're so dumb they forgot to lock us up."

Mary was very surprised but quickly regained herself. "Let's go, kids, but quietly." They nodded and filtered out of the room.

Mary led them through the castle quickly. Amethyst had no

idea how but somehow Mary knew her way through the castle. In a minute they were back on the courtyard. Soon, the castle was far away.

Breaking the silence, McKenna said proudly, "I knew all along they were dummies."

Amethyst asked hopefully, "So, we're going to rescue Miranda now?"

"I told you already- we need to find the ring first," said Mary.

Amethyst pouted. "But, the evil fairies will find her," she argued, staring at the wet grass they were tromping across.

"And then we'll rescue her with help from the ring," promised Mary. "You don't realize how dumb they are, Amethyst. They do the least important things first and save the really important stuff for last."

"I *told* you they were dummies," repeated McKenna.

As they were walking, Mary heard a small squeak under her feet. She quickly looked around to see if anyone else had heard it. But no one had. She stopped walking and bent down to inspect the ground.

"Mary!" Amethyst rushed over. "Are you alright?"

"I'm fine, honey cake," said Mary, but she didn't get up. She traced a faint outline of a square that was around her feet. *A trapdoor, cleverly designed by Mahalia to trap them.*

Mary heard it creak again. The wood under the grass, the door of the trapdoor, definitely wasn't walked on much, and now that weight was suddenly on it, it wasn't going to withstand long. A few minutes and it would cave in. Mary stood up, thinking. If she got off the square, she knew it would cave in on her as she pushed to get off. Either way they had her. But what would Amethyst think? Amethyst would be terrified out of her wits. Mary considered as Amethyst stared at her. It would definitely build up Amethyst's courage. Mary made her decision. *I'd better warn her best I can.*

"I have a promotion to make," said Mary, waiting for snap that would say the wood was about to give way. "If I am ever captured, I am making Amethyst-" There it was, the quiet snap.

She had less than two minutes left until she was once more a prisoner. "I am making Amethyst the leader."

"But...you'll never be gone, Mary," said Amethyst, confused.

"But what if something happens? This group will need a leader that will lead them to success in finding the ring."

A snap sounded, loud this time. Mary knew it was one of the main planks breaking. Everyone heard it. McKenna commented, "Well, I didn't know grass snapped. I thought it only grew."

A few seconds later the wood gave way and Mary shot straight down.

Amethyst screamed. And then all was quiet.

Courtney cast a fearful glance around. "We better get off the courtyard, Amethyst. What if there's lots of trapdoors around? What if~"

Amethyst didn't need to hear anymore. Taking one last look at the hole which had swallowed up their leader, she boldly took command and led her friends out of the dangerous courtyard.

chapter fourteen
Lucy is Startled

Queen Mahalia snarled at the helpless little girl cowering in the dingy room corner.

The little girl's name was Lucy, and between fits of crying she said, "Let me go, super-duper-ugly lady!" She was only six years old but had a very stubborn spirit.

Mahalia snorted. "Why would I? No way."

"Why?" asked Lucy. She hiccuped. "You're a meanie."

"So I am," said Mahalia with satisfaction. She glanced at herself in a large mirror on the wall and frowned. "Stop your nasty crying," she directed. "Your red face is ruining my reflection."

Lucy hiccuped twice, and tried her best to stay quiet. *How did this happen? One minute I'm a poor orphan locked in an asylum back room, and the next minute I'm locked in a dingy cellar with only an evil fairy for company?*

Just then Mahalia swirled and pointed an accusing finger at

Lucy. "I told you to quit crying,"she accused.

"I did," said Lucy innocently.

"Then get rid of your red face!" cried Mahalia, "or I'll tell Eugenia!"

Lucy quickly nodded, and then asked: "Could I see a bathroom, maybe, to wash my face?"

"No!" crowed Mahalia. "I can see through your plan, ugly one! You're trying to escape!"

"But how can I get the red off my face unless I can wash it?" asked Lucy.

"Rub it!" cried Mahalia. "Rub it on your shirt. Or leave it. I don't care. I'm leaving. Eugenia has summoned me. Goodbye, ugly one." And with that, she left the room, and locked it.

Lucy sank back in the corner. When would Amethyst ever come? Would they ever? She sighed, and closed her eyes.   Maybe she could get in a little nap......

Click.

The door's handle woke Lucy from her doze. She opened her eyes and shrieked as she felt Mahalia's hands on her shoulders. She attempted to scramble away but it did no good.

What was going on?

Lucy looked up and was horrified. Mary was being forced down to the cellar! Was everybody captured now? Was there any hope? Why was their leader in chains?

Only Mary was forced into the room and Lucy was relieved Amethyst, at least, was safe. At first Mary didn't notice her. She was poking her finger absentmindedly through a hole in her shirt and breathing heavily. She had her eyes closed.

"Mary?" Lucy's voice was barely above a whisper.

Mary's eyes flew open. "Lucy! Are you alright?" She scooted over and gave the little girl a hug.

She nodded wordlessly. "But Mary.... are you? And is Amethyst okay?"

"They're fine," promised Mary. "I'm just... a little confused. This was totally unexpected for me!"

chapter fifteen
Meet the Mochas

We're supposed to look in a big city, and I think Rome's out," said Josh. "It's Rome Street we want."

"I knew that," said Amethyst. "Let's see if we can find a map of this city."

Josh frowned. "Mary isn't here. We could rescue Miranda first."

Amethyst frowned too. "Mary told me specifically to search. I want to find Miranda twice as much as you'll ever want to, but I need to follow Mary's orders."

Rachel said, "Is that weird guy over there selling maps?"

Amethyst followed the little girl's gaze. There was an old man sitting on the sidewalk holding a newspaper. There were newspapers piled around him.

"No, Rae-Rae, that's a newspaper guy. And it's not nice to call people names, unless they're 100% evil. But good eyes, girl."

"That reminds me, we're probably going to need to buy a map," sighed Courtney, "and we're all broke."

"If we found somebody trustworthy," suggested McKenna, "we could ask to use their computer."

"The problem is, Kenna," said Emily, "we don't know who's trustworthy and who's not."

"It's McKenna," corrected McKenna. "And Amethyst, you found Mary, and she's trustworthy."

"That was before I knew evil fairies lurked around the area in disguise," said Amethyst.

"Awesome!" said McKenna. "We'll just pretend we don't know Mahalia and the others exist, and we'll find someone, *pronto!*"

"McKenna, that's not going to work," said Josh. "Because Mahalia and the others *do* exist."

"Let's just go," said Angelica, who was getting tired of arguing, "and when we find someone, we'll decide for ourselves. There's *only* four evil fairies."

"We only *think* there's four evil fairies," corrected Amethyst. "There could be a billion more." She was getting sick of arguing too, so she announced the quest's beginning, and they marched into the town in search of a kind person.

Soon they saw a family outside a rather large house. A woman was rocking on a porch swing, reading. She had silky brown hair and had a blue dress on.

A man was raking leaves out front. He had black hair and ripped jeans.

Two twin little boys, probably seven years old, were playing catch with a bright red ball. They both had blue eyes and blonde hair, and wore overalls and gym shoes.

A teenage girl lay in the grass by the boys, playing with a little baby in a fluffy pink dress. She had a blonde hair, too, but brown eyes, and had a sweatshirt on with jeans.

"Do they look trustworthy?" whispered Angelica.

Amethyst blinked. "Yes, I guess."

The woman spotted them. "Hello, children!" Her voice was soft. "Having a nice walk this evening?"

"Yes," said Amethyst. It was partly true. She walked up into the driveway to meet the woman, who had come down to say hello. "I'm Amethyst, and these are my sisters, Rachel and Emmy. And these are my friends, Josh, Angelica, Emily, Courtney, and McKenna."

"Nice to meet you," said the woman, offering her hand. "I am Jenny Mocha. You may call me Jenny."

"Mocha?" asked McKenna. "Like the coffee?"

The woman's laugh was low and soft. "Yes, like the coffee. This is my husband, Bob, and our kids." She motioned to the children. "These are the twins, Steve and Andrew, and this is our responsible teen Avery. And that's Katie, the baby."

"Hello," said Avery. For some reason, Amethyst noticed she seemed to recognize them.

"Is there anything we can get you?" asked Jenny.

"Uh," Amethyst thought they were trustworthy. "We kind of need a place to stay the night."

"You can stay," invited Mr. Mocha. "We have a decently big house. How many of you?"

Amethyst counted. *Herself, Angelica, McKenna, Courtney, Emily, Rachel, Emmy, Josh.....* "Eight, counting myself."

"Eight," mused Jenny. "Okay, Avery, you'll share with Katie, Amethyst, and her sisters. Josh, do you mind sharing with Steve and Andrew?"

"No," said Josh uncomfortably.

"Angelica, Courtney, McKenna, and Emily, do you mind sharing?"

"No," they said.

Amethyst didn't like being split up, but she didn't want to be rude. "Thank you for your hospitality."

"No worries, Miss Butternut," replied Jenny. "Follow me."

Amethyst frowned inwardly. *She had never told Jenny her last name. How did Jenny know?*

She followed Avery up to the second story. Avery showed her her room. It was painted bright red with hearts on the walls and on the bedspread. "You can sleep with me in the bed," she said, "and your sisters will sleep on the floor."

Amethyst said, "Can I sleep on the floor with my sisters?"

Avery looked uncomfortable. "My mom says I need to be

kind. I'll get in trouble if she finds out you're sleeping on the floor."

"Then I'll tell her I asked you." Suddenly the reason they were here struck Amethyst. "Could I use your computer? We need a map of the city."

"Uh," said Avery. "Yea.... come on downstairs. My mom'll get you set up."

Amethyst followed Avery downstairs. With Avery acting so weird and Jenny knowing her last name, she was beginning to reconsider her decision to spend the night. But if they didn't, where else would they stay? *It'll just be the night,* Amethyst decided. *We'll stay here just long enough to sleep, and we'll get on our way in the morning.*

When they got downstairs, however, Jenny was just laying dinner out on the table. "Perfect timing, you two," she said. "You're just in time for dinner. Chicken on the bone, mashed potatoes, green beans, biscuits, corn-on-the-cob, and chocolate cupcakes for dessert."

Amethyst's mouth watered.

"Doesn't it sound yummy?" cried Emmy, running over to Amethyst and hugging her leg. "Miss Jenny already gave us some hot cocoa. It was the best hot cocoa I ever tasted!"

Amethyst giggled nervously and hugged the little girl back. "Did you both have some?"

"Yea," said Rachel. "And guess what? Jenny said if I want I can have the biggest helping of mashed potatoes!"

Amethyst still didn't feel comfortable enough to eat the mouth-watering food. But she didn't want to appear rude. She looked around desperately for Angelica. Maybe they could discuss some things. McKenna would get too loud, Courtney was too serious, and Emily wasn't the talkative type. Of course she had Josh, but she didn't want to look like she had a boyfriend.

She turned and saw them all sitting at the table. She sat herself down besides Angelica and when Jenny had gone back into the kitchen to get the milk, she whispered, "Do you feel comfortable here?"

"No," said Angelica. "Let's talk later, though. We don't

want to appear suspicious. Should we eat this food?"

"As long as they eat it, too, we should be fine. Just don't pick up something to eat if they haven't touched it, no matter how much you love it."

Angelica nodded and repeated the message to the other girls while Amethyst told the little girls. "And if you need to, be 'full,'" she said.

Jenny came back into the room and they all sat down.

* * * * * * * * * * * * * * * * * * *

"Alright, who wants mashed potatoes?" Mr. Mocha held up the bowl. "I'm definitely getting some." He scooped some onto his plate, and Amethyst marked the potatoes as safe.

"I'll have some, please," said Amethyst, and when he gave her a scoop of potatoes she said thank you.

After everyone had been served it happened that there were two things the Mochas did not touch: the green beans and the biscuits. Everyone remembered and no one ate any.

Towards the end of the meal Avery noticed the untouched biscuits and green beans and winced. "I made the biscuits."

"No, I did," said Jenny, looking her daughter severely in the eyes. "Don't lie to me, young lady, or you'll be *severely* punished."

Amethyst's heart nearly stopped. Was it just a coincidence that the Mochas emphasized their *severely*'s, just like Miss Odelia?

"Sorry, Mom, I must be remembering last night." Avery winced, as if it was Jenny who was lying, not Avery. "I don't like those- yours. Why didn't you let me bake them?"

Now Mr. Mocha looked at his daughter. "You must remember the baking contest," he said. "You want your mother to win, don't you?"

Amethyst had trouble breathing. Why were they all acting so weird? Should they leave? But if they did, where'd they go?

"Anybody want seconds, or can I bring out dessert?" asked

Jenny. "I'm personally too full to eat any cupcakes, but I'm sure you guys aren't."

"I'm way too full, too," said Mr. Mocha, "and the twins are allergic to gluten so they can't have any. And of course Katie is too little."

Is it just me, thought Amethyst, *or are all the Mochas trying to avoid eating the cupcakes?*

"Avery, you want one?" Jenny offered a delicious chocolate cupcake to her daughter.

"No," said Avery in a small voice. "I- I- I just learned from my doctor appointment I'm lactose intolerant."

If Avery is so lactose-intolerant, why did she try to take credit for making biscuits with dairy in them?

Amethyst felt sick as a cupcake was placed in front of her.

"No, thank you," she said politely. "I'm very full as well."

"Aw, will somebody eat a cupcake?" asked Jenny.

"We're all too full, but we honor your hospitality," said Courtney.

Mr. Mocha's voice became serious. "Thank you. Now it is time for bed. You need a good night's sleep. Everyone, even us."

Amethyst obediently got up and took Emmy's and Rachel's hands. "Come along, girls." They went upstairs and while Avery and her brothers were in the bathroom Amethyst snuck over to Angelica's room.

"When Jenny showed us this room," whispered Angelica, "she was like, 'Here's your room, kids, and whatever you do don't touch the window, and don't get out without us giving you permission because there's a hole underneath one of the floorboards by the door and we don't want you getting hurt.' What did Avery say?"

"She said I could sleep in the bed with her," said Amethyst, "and when I asked if I could sleep on the floor, she got all uncomfortable and said she'd get in trouble for not having me in the bed."

"What will you do?" asked Angelica. "As for us, we're just going to sleep where she tells us and not obey the 'don't go out without us' rule."

"I'll probably ask Jenny for a map," said Amethyst, "and if she says no, or ignores me, I'll go searching myself."

"That is the whole reason we're here, right?" asked Angelica worriedly. "Every time we bring it up, they have an excuse not to do it- 'it's dinner time,' 'it's bedtime,' 'let's get you settled in first.' It's super-weird."

"What is?" asked Avery, coming into the room. "Amethyst, it's your turn for the bathroom. I already helped your sisters brush their teeth. There's a new tube of toothpaste on the sink you guys can use. Don't worry, we haven't touched it."

Amethyst caught Angelica's eye and gave her a warning glance. Angelica nodded very faintly.

Amethyst went into the bathroom and closed and locked the door. She ignored the slightly dented toothpaste bottle on the sink, meant for them, and searched for the toothpaste the Mochas used.

She found a squeezed tube of toothpaste behind the bottle of mouthwash in the cabinet.

Hm, should I use the toothbrush she gives me?

Amethyst replaced the tube and pulled out the mouthwash. She'd rinse her mouth. *But what if the mouthwash was bad?*

She replaced the mouthwash. What would she do? She could use Avery's toothbrush, but that would be... well... too gross.

Knock! Knock! "Amethyst, hurry up," called Steve. "I need to brush."

How could she make her teeth looked brushed when she hadn't brushed them? She scavenged the cabinet until she found it. A packaged toothbrush. She read the description and it didn't say anything like "Poisoned toothbrush." She pulled it out, threw the package in the trash, and brushed her teeth. Then she washed her brush, threw away the other toothbrush they had left, and put the new one where the old one had been. Then she left the bathroom and headed to Avery's room.

Avery was already in bed and Emmy and Rachel were snuggled on the floor with blankets and pillows. "Guess what, big sissy?" cried Emmy. "Avery brushed our teeth!"

"That's awesome," said Amethyst, bending down to kiss them. She pulled away. *Ugh!* What was that horrible smell on their breath? "What did you guys eat?"

"Same you did," said Rachel. "But the toof-past was yummy, too. It tasted like strawberries!"

"Good," said Amethyst. She climbed into the bed, not even bothering to get in pj's. Avery turned out the light and Amethyst snuggled down.

What if the bed was poisoned or something?

It couldn't be. Avery was in the bed. Amethyst took a deep breath and fell into a deep, deep, deep, dreamless sleep.

chapter sixteen
What's up with the Mochas?

Wake up, sleepyhead, breakfast time." Avery shook Amethyst awake.

"Uh... uh...what?" mumbled Amethyst. She wasn't ready to wake up yet. She wanted to sleep longer.

"Breakfast," said Avery, exasperated. "Emmy and Rachel are already down, eating."

"Igetsmsup," mumbled Amethyst. She sat up and rubbed her eyes. Suddenly she felt wide-awake. What was going on?

"Come on, you're the last one up," whined Avery, so Amethyst got up, rubbed her eyes again, and stumbled downstairs and sat at the table.

"Any eggs, sweetheart?" asked Jenny to Emmy. Amethyst blinked. Were eggs bad? But then she saw something yellow on Mr. Mocha's plate. She closed her eyes. So everything was fine.

She sat down.

"Yea," said Emmy, "and Rae-Rae wants some too."

Jenny smiled warmly at Amethyst. "Well, good morning, Amethyst. Sleep well?"

"Yes," said Amethyst. She spotted toast. That was her favorite. The Mochas had toast, too, so she helped herself to some.

"Like toast, Amethyst?" asked McKenna. "'Cause I love toast."

"Yep," said Amethyst, "did you sleep well?"

"No," said McKenna honestly. "The floor was too creaky, Angelica was snoring too loudly, and the window kept moving in the wind."

"I'm sorry about that, honey," said Jenny soothingly. "My husband'll fix that right up and you'll be all set for tonight."

"Huh?" asked Amethyst, picking at her toast. "We don't live here. After we get a map of the city, we'll be right on our way."

"But you're only children," pointed out Jenny. "Little kids like you shouldn't be needing a city map."

"It's for our parents," said Courtney quickly.

Mr. Mocha eyed them. "If you have parents, why did you need to spend the night?"

Amethyst thought quickly. "Uh, we were supposed to spend the night at a friend's, while our parents were out at a party, but it turned out our friends weren't home and we'd get in huge trouble if we disturbed their party."

"Interesting," said Jenny, "very interesting. So why do you need a city map for your parents?"

What a big mess they had gotten into. "One thing our dad really wants is a map, and if we get it for him we'll not get into as much trouble," said Josh.

Avery perked up. "So you're all related? I thought Amethyst said they were her *friends*!"

"I- they are," said Amethyst quickly. "They're my adopted sisters and brother. We just adopted them a few weeks ago so I still can't remember they're my sisters and brother, not friends. But Emmy and Rachel are my biological sisters." At least that much was true.

"Yes, yes," said Jenny slowly. "Avery, fetch a spare map."

Amethyst thought she saw Jenny wink.

"And we thank you for your hospitality," said Amethyst, pushing the table back.

Avery reappeared with a rolled-up map. "Here you go."

"Thanks, Avery," said Amethyst. She tucked the map in her waist belt and stood up, taking Emmy's and Rachel's hands. "Goodbye, Mochas, and thank you so much for your hospitality."

"You are welcome," said Jenny, and this time there was a familiar edge in her voice. For a second her eyes gleamed red, and then they turned back to their regular soft blue. "Goodbye, Butternuts."

There was that Butternut again, thought Amethyst. *How in the whole world did she know my last name?*

"And tell Mary hello from Jenny."

Amethyst's heart stopped. She screamed and ran out of the house as fast as her legs could carry her, with her sisters and friends trailing behind.

chapter seventeen
Marissa the Rag Doll

Cha-cha-cha," said Lucy. She danced around in a small circle. "Cha-cha-cha, pizza, in the cafeteria. Is that better?"

"Nope," said Mahalia. "You forgot the happy birthday part. And you have to *grooove*."

"Why do you even want a happy birthday sung to you from a poor little prisoner?" asked Lucy, frowning.

Because everybody else has sung it, and if you sing it right I'll break the record for the Person with the Most Happy Birthdays sung to, or whatever."

"Fine," said Lucy. Normally she loved singing, but this was different. "Happy birthday to you, cha-cha-cha...."

"You forgot the pizza part." Lucy sighed. She didn't want to do something that would win Mahalia any record. Maybe if she skipped a 'happy birthday'...yes, that would do. She started, "Happy birthday to you, Happy birthday dear-"

"You forgot the second verse!" cried Mahalia, outraged.

"Lucy," called Mary. "I suggest you do it right."

Lucy ignored Mary.

"Listen," said Mahalia. She pulled out her wand, which she had taken back from Mary. "This is the deal. You do it right, I'll reward you. You do it wrong, I'll punish you." Mahalia's punishments could be as interesting as the rewards, but more painful. Lucy decided that she would have to relent. She could attempt to skip a 'to' and just say "happy birthday you," but if Mahalia caught it she'd really get it. She sang it all the way through just about correctly.

"Perfect," said Mahalia. "Here." She waved her wand. A rag doll appeared. "There you go," she said as she left.

Lucy groaned and picked up the doll. She'd wanted something else, like something she'd be able to do, not a thing. But besides Mary, this doll was the only company she had. So she promptly named it Marissa.

"What's your doll's name?" asked Mary, moving over to Lucy.

"Marissa."

"Why?"

"I like the name."

Mary said, "I see."

Lucy studied the doll. She had button eyes and a drawn-on smile. She was stuffed with cotton and had yellow yarn hair braided into two pigtails. She had a blue dress and just arms and legs, no fingers or toes.

Lucy hugged the doll. "Mary, when will Amethyst come?"

"Soon, honey. Very soon. I promise."

"Have they found the ring yet?"

Mary glanced around. "I don't know, sweetie. All I know is, Amethyst loves me. And she loves you. So she'll be back."

Lucy just nodded and hugged Marissa even harder. If only she were a doll. Dolls had no worries because they were just stuffed with cotton.

chapter eighteen
A Very Peculiar Rubber Band

I'm tired, big sissy," said Rachel, her eyes drooping.

"Me too," said Emmy, and fell down and fell asleep right there on the concrete sidewalk.

Amethyst's heart raced. "They got a good sleep. What could they have done that would make them this tired?"

"They ate the hot cocoa and none of us did," said McKenna.

"They used the toothpaste we didn't use," said Emily.

Amethyst told herself, "Breathe, Amethyst." Then she picked Emmy carefully up and checked for a pulse. She was fine, breathing and looked like she was just sleeping.

In a minute's time Rachel fell too. McKenna caught her and put her into Josh's arms. "I'm too flimsy to hold a sleeping two-year-old that weighs seventy pounds."

Even though McKenna was wrong, Amethyst didn't feel like telling her the twins were four and weighed around thirty pounds.

"Let's just carry them until they wake up," suggested

Courtney.

"Angelica, will you get my map?" asked Amethyst. "Let's figure out where we need to go."

Angelica pulled the rolled-up map from Amethyst's pockets. She slowly removed the rubber band. She frowned and stretched it slowly between her fingers.

"Angelica, will you hurry up?" asked Amethyst in slight annoyance.

"Wait," said Angelica. "There's something very... *peculiar* about this rubber band. It feels weird."

Amethyst placed Emmy gently on the grass and walked over to Angelica, then grabbed for the rubber band. But as she did it slipped from her grasp and fell into a crack in the sidewalk. For a split second, right before it disappeared into the crack, Amethyst saw it sparkle. She gasped.

"What is it?" asked Josh, struggling under the weight he was carrying.

Amethyst didn't answer.

Courtney said, "Amethyst, what is it?"

Amethyst blinked. "Uh, uh.... oh, I, umm... nothing."

Courtney gave her a look.

"It's just...." said Amethyst, "I think...... that maybe was the ring....."

Everyone gasped.

"Why do you think that?" asked Courtney.

"It sparkled when it fell," said Amethyst. "Come, help me pry it up."

Josh placed Rachel on the grass, next to Emmy, and ran to help.

"Hey, what are you kids doing on my lawn?" called a nasty-sounding voice.

chapter nineteen
Dr. Sawyer

An old lady strode out on the pathway to where they were, on the sidewalk. "That's my lawn."

"We're on the sidewalk," pointed out Josh, "not the lawn."

"Same same. You're drawing nasty notes on the sidewalk with chalk, aren't you? You're some of those nasty kids who go around writing signs on people's sidewalks that say 'You're a horrible guy.'"

Amethyst quickly stood up. "No, we just.... thought we saw something we lost."

"Can you give me an explanation of why two little girls- pests, it looks like- are lying in my lawn, then?"

Amethyst quickly thought of something. "They fell asleep and we had to put them down to look. Can we go on looking please?"

"What did you lose, and what do you think you found?" asked the lady suspiciously.

"Uh, uh, a ring," said Amethyst. "A plastic little ring. It was my sister's, and she's addicted to it." Amethyst gestured to Emmy and tried to look desperate. "She'll really get mad and maybe even hurt us if she doesn't find this ring."

The lady said her name was Mrs. Mia and they could look as long as they didn't dig up the grass. "And if you can't find it within the hour, stop and come back tomorrow!"

Amethyst nodded. "Thank you, Mrs. Mia." She was relieved she could call an adult *Mrs.* instead of their first name.

Josh had one last question. "Do your kids call you *Momma Mia?*"

"No," said Mrs. Mia. She looked hurt. "Farewell, kids, and you'd better be out of here before the next hour, or you'll be *severely* punished."

Is it just the way people say it, thought Amethyst, *or does Mrs. Mia and Jenny both know and are with Miss Odelia?* She was worried either way, and felt uncomfortable. *We won't even go in the house,* she promised herself. *We'll just stay out front in the lawn.*

They worked for a long time, taking turns sticking their fingers into the cracks (Mostly McKenna- she insisted her fingers were "skinny and made for going in cracks").

"Has it been an hour yet?" asked Angelica, standing up and stretching her arms.

Amethyst frowned. "If it hasn't been it'll be soon. Let's go. We'll come back tomorrow, like Mrs. Mia said, and this time with an explosive or something."

"An explosive?" Courtney looked at Amethyst funnily. "Are you feeling okay, Amethyst?"

"I'm fine... I just was daydreaming I guess," said Amethyst. She bent down and lifted Emmy off the ground. "Uhhhh. I wonder if Mrs. Mia knows a doctor?"

"I'll ask," said McKenna cheerfully and skipped up to the door.

While they were waiting, Amethyst tried to look into the crack, but it was no use. She stuck her fingers down into it, and felt it, but trying to grasp it was useless.

She looked up to see McKenna skipping back down the path just as cheerfully. "She said, 'You're really rude kids to ask a poor old lady that, but the doctor around the corner's mighty good. I brought my kid there once for a broken bone.' Is that helpful?"

"It sure is," said Courtney, "he's probably a bone -"

Amethyst rolled her eyes- why did Courtney have to be so against McKenna all the time? "McKenna, that's perfect. All we need," she said. "Don't listen to her."

McKenna shot Courtney a triumphant glance. Courtney scowled.

With Angelica in the lead, they followed Mrs. Mia's instructions and went around the corner. Sure enough, a big building labeled DR. SAWYER was there. When they entered, a little bell rang. The clerk looked up.

"What can I do for you kids? Are you lost?"

"No," said Josh. He spoke for all of them. "Uh, my friend's sisters, Emmy and Rachel-" He gestured to the sleeping figures- "they had a really good sleep and they suddenly fell asleep this morning, and they've barely woken up since then."

"Where are your parents?" asked the clerk. She was scribbling things on a piece of paper.

"Uh, we're orphans," said Angelica quickly.

"Why aren't you at an asylum? There's one around here. I see what you did. Kids escape all the time and come here. Well, we won't help you. The asylum has a good doctor there as well."

No! We can't be put back in the asylum! Amethyst had trouble breathing. "Please, please, please, please do not send us back there. We have slop for food and-" she sniffled- "and no heating except in classrooms. And the mistresses.... they're the worst thing you can imagine!"

"Liars," said the clerk.

"Hey Lexi," said a low voice, and a doctor emerged from a nearby office. "What's all this name-calling?"

"Escaped kids," was all Lexi said.

"I don't care if they're escaped criminals. You're my daughter, and I won't have you calling names. Now what do you need, kids?"

Amethyst repeated their request.

"Sleepers, eh? Well, follow me." He led them to a room and

93

had them lay the sleeping girls on two beds. "This isn't a hospital but I can treat them no problem."

He looked them over. "Where have you kids really been?"

Amethyst hesitated, and then it spilled out. She told everything, starting at leaving the asylum and ending with Emmy and Rachel falling asleep. She left out the part about the ring.

The doctor nodded at the end. "Very reasonable explanation. There's more and more horrible happenings these days. I'm sorry if my daughter-clerk was rude to you. She used to be quite nice, but ever since....." He stopped, his eyes looking dreamy. But then he snapped back into focus. "Well, it looks like to me they have unconsciousitis."

"Unconsciousitis?" repeated Emily. "What's that?"

"A disease only caused on purpose where the victim is unconscious in sleep and wake, and can be persuaded to do anything. It can be cured but only very carefully. Do you mind if I keep and take care of your sisters while you continue your journey?"

Amethyst didn't want to leave her sisters. But she knew it might be the only way they would be better. And besides she'd be putting them all in danger if she brought them along because who knew what Eugenia'd make them do if they were captured?

Amethyst wanted to laugh, but she didn't have anything to laugh about, so she whispered to McKenna, "Tell him we're fine with leaving them for a bit." *There. Now McKenna will make it really funny and I'll get to laugh with everybody else.*

McKenna looked at her funny. But she said, "Whatever-your-name-is, Amethyst wants you to know we're fine with leaving them here. By the way I have no idea why she won't say it herself."

"Shy?" asked the doctor. "Maybe it's because you haven't heard my name. I'm Dr. Sawyer.... uh, Smumble."

Automatically, Amethyst said, "I'm Amethyst Butternut, and these are my friends, Angelica, McKenna, Courtney, Emily, and Josh."

"And Avery," came an unmistakable voice from outside, and then Avery Mocha barged inside the building.

chapter twenty
The Return of Avery Mocha

What are *you* doing here?" said McKenna. She put her hands on her hips and narrowed her eyes, slowly advancing on Avery.

"Um... Can we go outside?"

Amethyst frowned. "We do have to go now anyhow. Thanks, Dr. Sawyer. We'll be back another time for them."

"One thing.... who do I call if you don't come back?" asked Dr. Sawyer.

Amethyst frowned. "Uh, find Mary Littles. She's very nice."

"Okay," said the doctor but sounded unsure.

Amethyst followed Avery outside.

Avery said, "Can I please have that map back, Amethyst? My mom was so mad at me because I gave you the wrong map."

Amethyst was surprised. She took the map from Angelica and

handed it over. "The rubber band's gone, but here's the map."

Avery took a deep breath. "I've- uh- also come to apologize. My family is, uh, well.... evil. I'm sorry. I knew it was wrong, but my mom forced me to. But I realized I needed to get your forgiveness." Tears spilled from her eyes. "I'm so, so, so, so sorry!" She wiped her eyes on her sleeve.

"We forgive you," said Courtney gently.

A lightbulb came on in Amethyst's head. "Avery? Can I ask you a bizarre question?"

Avery looked at her funnily. "Sure?"

"What street do you live on?"

Avery thought for a moment. "Uh, Rome Street?"

Amethyst could hardly keep from shouting "Yes!" The ring was located on Rome Street, which was where they had gotten the map from. And so that rubber band had to be the ring!

McKenna decided that all the wrongdoings Avery had done were not done anymore. "Let's-invite-her-to-go-on-the-quest," she sang.

"What quest?" asked Avery. "And I have to be back at my house soon or my mom will notice I'm gone and will come after me."

"Who are.... who are your mother's comrades?" asked Emily, after a moment's thought.

"I've never met them myself. I think one's name is Odelia?" Avery shrugged.

"I know Odelia," said Amethyst quietly. "She's the most evilest person I've ever met. I'm not friends with her, of course, but I've talked to her. She was the headmistress at my old asylum."

"And....and....your sisters..." choked out Avery.

"We know," said Josh gently. "They're in a doctor's care, as you know."

Beep, beep! Avery pulled out a cell phone. "I.... gotta go now, guys. I.... I...don't want to, but... but..."

"You don't have to," said Angelica. "Come with us, and you'll be able to rid yourself of your evil mother."

Avery yelled, "I don't want to rid myself of my mother! I want her to change!"

Amethyst sighed. "I'm not sure there's a chance of that happening, Avery. Please come with us."

Avery looked over her shoulder, as if she were afraid her mother was already coming. "Can I go back when I'm done?"

Amethyst nodded.

So that was how Avery joined their group.

As they walked, Amethyst explained everything to Avery, who made a solemn promise not to tell a soul.

"You're sure Steve and Andrew aren't nice, too?" asked Josh for the hundredth time as they walked along. Suddenly he looked up. "I found fruit!"

Soon they sat around an apple tree, munching on the yummy apples.

"Hey, Amethyst," said McKenna, juice dribbling down her chin, "how will we get that ring-rubber-band up? Argghha!" she yelped, suddenly, as she realized the dribbling juice was staining her already-stained clothing.

"You should be glad it isn't a rip," murmured Courtney.

"For your question... I'm not sure. Maybe if we had a hook, we could stick it down there and pry it up."

"Yea..." said McKenna. "A really long, hooky hook that specializes in grabbing rubber bands out of slim sidewalk cracks!"

"Good idea," commented Angelica.

"Some idea," scoffed Courtney. "We'd never be able to find that type of hook."

"Courtney...." warned Amethyst.

Avery looked at Amethyst. "Do they always fight like this?"

Amethyst nodded, and rolled her eyes.

"Okay," she said. "We'll get a good night's sleep, and then get searching for that really, really long hooky hook."

Courtney opened her mouth but then shut it. McKenna looked pleased. She smiled happily in Amethyst's direction.

And they settled down to sleep under the tree~ even though it was only six o'clock~ as they were all exhausted.

In the morning when Amethyst woke up she saw Avery staring at her. "What is it?" she asked worriedly.

Avery shrugged. "Nothing."

"You look bored," said Amethyst. She rubbed her eyes and smoothed her ragged purple dress. "Why?"

"I don't know. I'm not as tired as all of you. I'm used to waking up bright and early."

"Good morning, y'all!" McKenna sat straight up and wiggled her toes. "How's it going, girlfriend?"

Amethyst rolled her eyes happily. "Nothing much. I just woke up. Did you get a good night's sleep?"

"Sure did," said McKenna. "At least I got better sleep here than y'all. I saw Courtney wake a good seven times, but I slept whole night through."

"That's impossible," said Avery. "If you slept the whole night, you would've never known Courtney was up."

"Oops." McKenna clamped a hand to her mouth. "Sorry 'bout that, girlfriend. Now can I wake up Courtney?"

"Don't you even think about it," said Courtney from under the pile of leaves where she had been sleeping. "I'll never forgive you."

"Well sorry for worryin' you there, girlfriend," said McKenna. "I just woke up, ya see. I woke before y'all." She climbed on top of the leaf pile.

"Aowaoaw!" Courtney squealed and jumped out of the pile. She brushed herself off. "Leave me alone! And cut the accent while you're at it!"

"What's wrong with a good old California accent?" said McKenna.

"It's not a California accent," said Amethyst as gently as she could. "I'm not quite sure what it's called."

"But I can still talk in it, right, girlfriend?" asked McKenna hopefully.

"Unless you want Courtney at you you'd better stop," advised Avery. "I've seen enough to know she can get pretty nasty."

"Hey!" said Courtney angrily.

"Stop it you two," said Amethyst. She sighed. "McKenna, wake up Angelica *gently* and please don't use your accent, unless you want Courtney to be mad at you. Courtney, *please* try not to annoy McKenna. Wake up Josh, please, and I'll wake up Emily."

After everyone was awake Josh and Amethyst gathered apples from the tree above and passed them around. After everybody had had their fill, they began to discuss how to retrieve the ring.

"I really like McKenna's idea," said Amethyst, "even though I'm not sure where we'll find such a hooky hook."

"What if we didn't stick a *hook* down the hole, but a *stick*?" suggested Angelica.

Amethyst thought for a moment. "I guess it's worth a try. Everybody take an apple for lunch and let's set out."

They did just that, and, after stopping quickly by Dr. Sawyer's to check up on Emmy and Rachel (who had not improved), they headed towards Mrs. Mia's.

"One thing," said Josh as they were nearing Mrs. Mia's house. "Where will we get sticks?"

McKenna rolled her eyes and walked in front of him. "Right here!" She pointed to a huge tree carefully decorating Mrs. Mia's landscape.

"Mrs. Mia will see us," groaned Angelica.

Luck was on their side, however, for at that moment Mrs. Mia exited their house with a purse. She got into her car and drove halfway down the driveway to where they were. She rolled down her window. "You nasty kids can look for your ridiculous ring while I'm gone. I'll be at the fair two hours away so I won't be back until dark." Then she drove away.

"What good luck," said Josh, staring unbelievably at the turn where Mrs. Mia's car had gone.

They looked at each other and raced to the tree, where they began to crack off small branches. In a minute they were all taking turns putting their stick down the hole, and nobody was succeeding.

After what had to been an hour of waiting-and-sticking-sticks-down-a-hole, Amethyst gently shoved McKenna out of the way and reached a new stick, a slim but sturdy one, into the little hole. She felt around desperately but felt nothing.

She stuck the stick down as far as she could reach, and this time, when she pulled it up, the little rubber band hung from it.

Everyone cheered.

But before Amethyst could take the ring-rubber-band off the stick, rough hands grabbed her waist. "Don't you even *think* about taking that ring!" said Jenny Mocha.

chapter twenty-one
Attack!

Mom, please, they're my friends," begged Avery.

"Darling, you shouldn't be hanging out with these people. Besides, I already have backup."

Amethyst struggled. "How'd you-" She stopped, getting a glimpse of what was behind Jenny. The sight made her sick.

Mahalia, brandishing her ruby-tip wand, was there, her black hair braided twice as much around her body and probably five times as dirty and black. This time the dress she wore was red and covered in rubies. Her crown was as grimy as usual.

Eugenia was there, too, wearing a suit of silver armor with her dirty hair flying out around her silver mask. Miss Odelia and Miss Quiana were there, looking identical with flowing net-like blue dresses, buns in hairnets, and green shoes decorated with net and lined with net. They had blue-net sashes and piercing green eyes.

And Mrs. Mia was there. So *that* was where she had gone. Amethyst saw what their plan had been. Have the orphans find and dig up the ring and then claim it for themselves. Well, that wasn't about to happen if Amethyst had anything to do with it.

Miranda was out there, in need of rescue.

Amethyst struggled to get down to the ring. Josh had ducked

behind a bush and now jumped out and raced over to the ring (Amethyst was sure it was the ring now). He snatched it up and stuck it in his pocket right as Miss Quiana grabbed him. "Give - me - that - ring," she hissed.

Josh covered the pocket. "Let go of me!"

"Let's go, Joshy, let's go!" screamed McKenna from behind the arms of Miss Odelia. "Punch those meanies, make 'em cry!"

"Shush up, girl," hissed Miss Odelia. "It's not going to help."

"I don't care," said McKenna. "Punch, hit, or kick, whatever it takes to make 'em cry!"

Amethyst had a sudden idea, powered by McKenna's words. In one swift motion, she brought her hand up in a fist. Her fist hit its mark, and Jenny leaped back, holding her nose and howling in pain.

Amethyst wrung her hands. "Who's next?"

Like she suspected, everyone else was getting nervous, so nervous that many of them loosened their grips. Angelica slid out and ran to Amethyst along with Josh and Emily.

Eugenia stormed to the front, dragging Courtney. "It's no use against *magic*," she said, and pulled out her wand.

Amethyst closed her eyes.

But just at that moment a *wheeop!* split the air. A fast-moving kicking boy bounded into the area. He kicked his way to Eugenia and launched his foot into Eugenia's wand.

"Steve!" shouted Josh.

"I'm not on your side," said Steve Mocha. "I'm just, let's say giving you a head start, you know, to get you going."

"Good enough," said Josh. He silently and secretly passed Amethyst the ring, which was now in the shape of a ruby necklace.

Still not an amethyst, thought Amethyst disappointingly. She placed it in her ragged pocket and Josh joined Steve in battling Eugenia.

Courtney had escaped and was huddling fearfully behind Amethyst. "W-w-w-w-will-lll e-e-everything b-b-b-e ok-kay?" she stammered fearfully. "I-i-is e-e-everybody o-okay?"

Amethyst looked at Courtney funny. "We've been captured

before and you never were this fearful."

"Last time we came from great heights," said Courtney, sounding like McKenna. "The fall knocked the fear right out of me."

Amethyst rolled her eyes and went back to watching the "battle," waiting to come in if she needed to.

"I-i-i-is M-m-McK-kenna o-okay?" hiccuped Courtney.

Amethyst had not been expecting this at all. How could she? Courtney was against McKenna in many, many ways.

But still, Amethyst scanned the battlefield. "Well, she's still in Miss Odelia's grip, but she's punching her a whole lot so she should get free soon. Why do you care?"

Courtney hiccuped again. She didn't say a word.

At that moment McKenna *did* break free. She punched Miss Odelia one last time for good measure and then rushed over and grabbed Amethyst. "You okay, you okay, you okay, you okay?" she said in one breath. "I'm fine, fine, fine, fine."

"Good," said Courtney quietly.

McKenna looked at her, startled. "Is that supposed to be a joke?"

"No," said Courtney.

McKenna just stared at her. "Are you sure it isn't April first?"

"What's April first?" Courtney wanted to know.

"April Fools Day, duh!" said McKenna. "Last year when I was put on the train, y'know, I played a nasty trick on Eugenia. I said 'May I go potty?' and when she unfroze me I just stayed in the bathroom until she knocked on the door. Then I filled a small basket in there with soapy bubbles and opened the door, threw it on her face and yelled 'April Fools!' You should've seen her face!"

Amethyst giggled, picturing it. "That's an excellent trick, McKenna. Did she punish you for it?"

"Listen, guys," said Courtney, "we could sit around chatting all day but then we'd probably end up as prisoners. So let's fight, okay?"

They sighed and agreed. Amethyst made sure the Ring was in her pocket and went back to fighting against the evil people. Avery was sitting on the side, cowering. *She probably doesn't want to get in trouble with her mom,* thought Amethyst.

Soon everyone was free and lined up besides Amethyst. In front of them was the line of villains.

"Kids," said Mahalia. She stepped up. "I advise you: hand over the ring. If you hand it over, we won't capture you, and we'll let your little friends go. But if you don't, things will get nasty."

Amethyst knew Mahalia's words were as false as her beautiful looks. "Sorry, but I'm keeping it for now." She clamped a hand over her mouth. She should have said *We're keeping it!* Now all of them would know she had it!

"Troops," said Mahalia, still keeping her eyes on Amethyst, "get the ring or be *severely* punished."

Amethyst put one hand on her face and one over her pocket, and began to run backwards. McKenna, Courtney, Angelica, Emily, and Josh got in front of her, fighting back while she escaped. But where could she go where it was safe?

She saw a stream coming up. She could jump over it, or....

Amethyst jumped into the cold water. Still holding a hand over her pocket, she swam fast. She had never known how to swim, but now that her life and her friends' practically depended on it, she knew how. She ducked underwater and when she had been swimming for a minute she stopped and looked back, expecting Mahalia and Eugenia to be close at her heels.

Instead, her friends were flailing in the stream, swimming after her. All the villains were still on dry land, staring unbelievably at Amethyst. Then they started running along the side. *They must be afraid of water,* Amethyst decided. She ducked underwater and saw Josh coming up besides her. She reached into her pocket to give him the ring.... except there was no ring.

She hid her panic and motioned that it was lost to Josh. She went to the surface and gulped some air, and went back down, searching, searching for something floating in the currents.

In a bit everyone was helping, and apparently the villains had not even noticed the ring was missing yet.

Finally, Angelica spotted something shiny at the bottom of the stream and pointed it out to Amethyst, who dove down deeper. She grasped the shiny object and brought it up to the top of the stream to see what it was. Realizing Amethyst had the ring, Jenny dove on top of her, just as Amethyst realized it was a sparkly seashell, not the ring.

Suddenly she had a fantastic idea. She shook her head slightly at Josh to show it wasn't the ring, and then pretended the seashell was the ring. She held it tightly to her chest as if she were protecting it.

Jenny tried to pry Amethyst's hands up. Amethyst lifted her arm and threw the seashell far along the river. It landed with a small *splash* and sank.

Jenny yelled and got out of the stream. She ran to the spot where she saw what-she-thought-was-the-ring fall and dove underwater. Immediately she swam up, coughing and wheezing.

Amethyst took the opportunity- now was time to find the real ring. She swam down, looking carefully. Then she saw something sparkly. She reached down and grabbed it, and it was another seashell. *Drat.* If all sparkly things were seashells, they'd never find it!

Suddenly she heard a *glub-glubba-glub* sound, and saw Josh, still underwater, holding the ring. Not a sparkly seashell, but the real ring. Clearly he had forgotten he couldn't speak underwater and had tried to yell "I found it!" Slowly he swam to the surface, where he spat out a mouthful of water and winced. "Oops. But hey, I found the first crab!" he said to fool the fairies that were listening in.

"Good for you, but we need to focus on regaining our swimming skills so we can re-attack the fairies and get the ring," said Amethyst, also trying to fool the fairies.

Mrs. Mia, who had been listening, rushed over to the rest of the villains and said, "They haven't found the ring. They just found a crab, so don't worry!" Amethyst and Josh broke out in laughter. They all clambered out of the stream while nobody was looking and began to run back to the clearing.

Avery was still cowering under the tree. "Avery," said Amethyst. "Avery, it's alright. We have the ring."

Avery didn't say anything. Amethyst searched for words, but McKenna took over. "Well, be that way. We're not going to stick around for long. We've a journey ahead of us. If you want to sit and cower while we face all dangers, be my guest. We're not going to spend our time pitying over poor Avery when we should be rescuing Lucy and Mary."

For once, Amethyst agreed.

Avery got up slowly. "I can't go. My mom said I have to stay."

"But-" said Amethyst and then understood. Magic. "I'm sorry. Do you want me to free you with the ring?"

Avery shook her head. "I have to make my mom right first. Good luck, though." She stood up and began walking.

Amethyst rolled her eyes. "Thanks for staying on our side. Don't tell them we have it, and enjoy the scenery."

Avery didn't laugh. She just kept walking.

chapter twenty-two
Steve Mocha

Where y'all going?"

Josh turned around. "Huh? Oh, hi, Steve. We're just trying to find someplace to sleep. Thanks for giving us the head start."

"No problem," said Steve. "I was trained in karate, and as much as I enjoy being evil, I sorta liked you guys."

"Gee, thanks," said Josh.

"Not you," joked Steve. "Everyone else."

Josh's face became red. "Oh."

Steve rolled his eyes and gave Josh a playful punch. "I'm joking. Good luck on whatever you're doing. I'd help but I can't keep secrets, so if you found that magic ring my mom is always looking for, don't tell me, because I'll blurt it to them, I can guarantee you."

"Okay," said Amethyst. "Goodbye, Steve. Say hi to Andrew for Josh." She grinned.

Steve gave her a thumbs-up. "You got it, girl. 'Bye." He scampered away to join his sister.

"Don't you realize," said Amethyst as they trudged on, "that Avery and Steve are rather weird? Avery, one minute she seems honest, and the next she seems like a liar."

Josh nodded. "Yea... why?"

"I'm not sure if that means she's evil pretending to be nice or nice faking evil." Amethyst frowned.

"Yea, me neither," said Angelica. "So where do we go now?"

"I think we need to return it now, to where it goes," said Amethyst.

"But," said McKenna, "where *does* it belong?"

Amethyst stopped suddenly, causing everyone to fall down behind her. She slowly turned. "I have no idea. Do any of you remember what Mary said?"

"How could we?" asked Josh, getting up and rubbing his elbow. "It's not like we are fairies or anything."

"Think, everyone, *think*," said Amethyst, starting to walk again. "Where did Mary say it needed to go?"

"Hey," said Emily, realization dawning. "We can't return it yet!"

"Why not?" asked Amethyst, not really paying attention to Emily and trying to concentrate on remembering.

"We need it to rescue Mary and Lucy and Miranda," said Emily in exasperation. "I can't believe you forgot."

"I didn't," said Amethyst absentmindedly. "I remembered." But she kept on walking as if she hadn't heard.

"Amethyst? Did you hear me?" called Emily.

"What? Who? Oh, yes. I heard you. Now let's get going!"

"No!" everyone cried.

Amethyst turned around. "Huh?"

"You *didn't* hear me," Emily informed her. "We need the ring to rescue Mary, Lucy, and Miranda!"

"Oh!" Amethyst smacked herself on the forehead. "How could I forget? Please don't tell Mary! Will you promise not to? I'd be *sooo* embarrassed!"

"I can't promise anything," said Josh cheerfully. "Now, does anybody know what direction we must go in to reach Mahalia's castle?"

Amethyst frowned. "Hmm..... I'm actually not sure, and with the Jenny incident and the Mrs. Mia incident, I'm not sure I want to walk around asking strangers questions."

"I agree," said Courtney. "I wish we had Mahalia's wand with us, but Mary had it, and she was taken."

"I know," said Amethyst. "Well, is Mahalia's castle in this city?"

Nobody knew.

"Avery might know," suggested Angelica. "After all, her mom's with Mahalia."

"But the question is, can we safely find Avery without finding Jenny?" asked Emily.

Amethyst frowned again. "I don't know, probably not."

"Steve would know, too," said Josh slyly.

"He's not-" Amethyst paused and looked at Josh, who was grinning. "Josh? Is Steve following us?"

Crash, bang, shuffle! Steve Mocha dropped out of the tree they were walking under.

"Steve, are you good, or are you evil?" asked McKenna. "Because we don't want you if you're evil."

"McKenna!" cried Courtney, "that's rude!"

"If he's not on our side I'm going to be even more rude," said McKenna. "So? You'd better make up your mind soon. And unless you're nice, you'd better stop following us."

"I'm not evil," said Steve slowly, "but I can't say I'm nice."

"Like Avery," said McKenna without thinking.

"Avery's nice," said Steve. "Stop insulting my sister. Anyways, I'm not gonna turn you in, okay? I'll stay with you, though. Josh needs company, because I know girls can get pretty annoying." He winked at Josh.

"I guess I need company, but these girls aren't bad," admitted Josh. "Except for the fact that Courtney and McKenna fight a lot."

"Fighting? Who needs fighting? One more fight out of you, I'm turning you in," joked Steve, staring seriously at the two.

"Yes sir," they said together, and afterword McKenna said, "Jinx, you owe me a soda."

"Whatever," said Courtney. "I don't even know what that means."

"If we say the same thing at the same time," explained McKenna slowly, "the first person to say 'Jinx, you owe me a soda,' makes the other person owe her a soda."

"So I owe you a soda. Whatever. I don't even have a soda. Let's go," said Courtney.

"Fine, then you owe me *three* sodas," said McKenna, skipping along behind Courtney, who was walking boldly ahead. "And my favorite type is the McKenna type."

"There is no McKenna type," said Steve. "There's Sprite, 7-Up, Pepsi, root beer.... but no McKenna type."

McKenna pouted. "Get me Sprite then, Courtney, okay?"

"Whatever. I don't even know what Sprite is," said Courtney.

"Come troops, let's go. And please-" Her plead for McKenna to not chant was cut off by "Let's go, go, go, go, go!" from McKenna.

McKenna stopped. "What did you want to say, Honorable Courtney?"

"Nothing... just be a little quieter, okay, girl?" asked Courtney.

McKenna nodded.

Amethyst said to Steve, "Steve, do you know where Queen Mahalia's castle is?"

"Mahalia? You don't want to see *her*. Right now, she has 300 prisoners, and she'd take you prisoner easy as pie. But it's right over that hill." He pointed to a hill far off in the distance. "Once you get over that you'll see it. I would say it's a day's journey."

A day's journey, thought Amethyst. *Not too bad. We can do that.* "Thanks, Steve. And you can come along if you like."

Steve hesitated. "Nah. I was just followin' you to see where you were goin'. Now that I know you're goin' to Mahalia's castle, I don't need to follow y'all anymore. Any more questions 'fore I take off?"

Amethyst thought. She didn't find anything she needed to ask, so she told Steve thanks, we don't need anything. Steve nodded towards them and ran off, hopefully for good. Amethyst didn't like it much when Steve pretended to run off and then secretly followed them.

"Right over that hill, eh?" asked Josh. "We'll need food. I'm hungry."

"And water," added Angelica. "My mouth is dry."

Amethyst scratched her head. "Is there fruit in the tree above us? Courtney, come back!" she cried, realizing Courtney was far away now, thinking they were following.

Courtney turned, saw they were not following her, and ran back. "Sorry," she panted. "I thought we needed to go."

"No, not yet," said Amethyst.

"There's pears up here," said Josh, who had climbed the tree.

Pears have juice so we should be fine with just them, thought Amethyst. She told Josh to toss some down, and he did- right on her head!

"Ouch! Ow! Yow! Josh, not- oww! on me!" she yelped.

Josh climbed down. "Oops, sorry, Amethyst. Didn't mean to. Here are some fruits- handed to you," he added, handing her some mouth-watering pears.

Amethyst took one and sunk her teeth into it. Juice dribbled down her chin. "Delish."

"Hey, we want some, too!" said McKenna, coming up and stealing some pears. She took a bite.

Amethyst giggled. "Go ahead, take all you want. Josh, after you eat, please gather pears for our journey."

"What can we carry them in?" asked Courtney. "Drat, that should've been a question for Steve! 'Do you have any bags?' How did we not think of it?"

Amethyst shrugged. "I don't know. I guess we'll be stuck carrying the pears. Everybody except McKenna take five to hold."

McKenna pouted. "Why can't I hold the pears?"

Amethyst grinned. "Because you'd eat them before we would have a chance to see them."

McKenna pouted. "I wouldn't. I would only eat if I felt like eating."

Courtney rolled her eyes. "And how often is that?"

McKenna looked guilty. "Every five minutes, about."

Courtney grinned.

Angelica was doubtful. "If McKenna doesn't hold any we'll have five less pears."

Amethyst thought. Angelica did have a point. Amethyst could announce that the pears you held were the pears you were eating. Then if McKenna ate all of her pears before the day's end, Amethyst could tell her, Too bad, we told you to save them. But then what? McKenna would get hungry, and Amethyst didn't want to know what she would do when she got hungry, and besides she couldn't let one of her friends starve.

McKenna turned towards Amethyst. "Captain Amethyst? Are you on my side? Do you say I'm mature enough to hold a few pears?"

Amethyst looked at McKenna's face. She tilted her head sideways. McKenna had on the look of an innocent young girl.

"If I give you some pears to hold," said Amethyst, "will you be able to save them and make them last?"

McKenna kept her I'm-so-innocent look on. "Of course, Amethyst. I will only eat when you tell me to." Her voice sounded as innocent as her looks.

"Well," said Amethyst, "okay. But don't eat them all. That will be the pears YOU eat. Those are *your* pears. And even though they're yours, you can only eat them when we say."

McKenna stopped her happy dance. "You mean 'when *I* say.' I'm *not* taking any orders from Courtney." She stood defiantly.

Amethyst sighed and rolled her eyes. "Yes, that's what I meant. Now we'll camp out under these trees tonight and tomorrow we'll start our journey." She had suddenly noticed the darkening sky above them. "We need a good night's sleep."

McKenna gasped. "But if we stay *here*, Captain Amethyst, the bad guys will find us! I *guarantee* it!"

"McKenna has a point," admitted Emily.

"Then let's sleep in the tree branches," said Amethyst and started clambering up the tree. "We're not going anywhere tonight."

McKenna had a protest all ready, however. "No. Amethyst, sleeping in a *tree* is a *very* bad idea." She was very serious. "You could roll off the branches and break your legs and arms."

"Then sleep on the ground in plain sight," said Amethyst. She wanted to sleep now so they could get an early start the next day, and at this rate they'd never get there.

"Fine, but if I get hurt, you're to blame," said McKenna, climbing up onto a large tree branch.

"Whatever," said Amethyst.

"We'll start early?" asked Courtney and McKenna in unison accidentally, and unfortunately for the others, McKenna instantly sat up, pointed at Courtney, and declared, "*Ha!* Now you owe me *four* sodas!"

"What*ever*," sighed Courtney, her usual response. "Now go to sleep."

"Fine, then," said McKenna as usual. "You now owe me *five* sodas."

"I don't even *have* five sodas," sighed Courtney in exasperation.

Amethyst said, "Quit it, you two. As an answer, yes, everybody, we'll start early." She checked her pocket to make sure the ring was there, and then, exhausted, fell asleep.

chapter twenty-three
The Plan

Amethyst woke to birds chittering. She opened her eyes and it took her a moment to remember where she was. And then it came back to her.

"And sorry, McKenna, but I can't get you ANY sodas, ever." Courtney grinned at McKenna from her sleeping branch.

McKenna's mouth opened in shock. "But Courtney, I jinxed you! And it's the rule- you have to give me at least one soda! I've never, ever had a soda!"

"Neither I," snapped Courtney, rather meanly. "And I dreadfully want one."

Amethyst sighed, pulled the ring out of her pocket to make sure it was there and then put it back, and said, "Everyone gather five pears each and let's begin."

They did so, and, with Amethyst in the lead, started out. By the time they reached the top of the hill they had only one pear left, it was mid-afternoon, and, according to McKenna, Courtney now owed her twenty-five sodas. (Of course Courtney ignored her every time.)

"Jinx, jinx, jinx, jinx, jinx, jinx," said McKenna happily.

"Courtney, you now owe me thirty-one sodas. And all Sprite."

"Whatever," said Courtney. "How close are we, Amethyst?"

Amethyst looked up, and she could barely make out the outline of Mahalia's castle.

"A couple miles away," said Amethyst, pointing it out to Courtney.

They traveled another hour, then Amethyst had everyone eat their last pears.

Amethyst was about to call a huddle to explain their plan when she glanced up and saw the sky. It was beginning to get dark.

"So, Amethyst, what's the plan?" asked Angelica.

Amethyst made a decision. "Actually, guys, it's getting dark. We'll do the plan tomorrow, when we have more light and more time. If we did it now we'd first have to deal with getting a light, then not getting tired."

"Okay," Angelica said. She yawned. "I'm tired anyway."

Amethyst looked around and saw a tree. She really didn't want to sleep in a tree again but there was really no other choice. Besides, if they slept anyplace else, they would be fully visible from the castle. She announced this to the group and mostly everyone was okay with it, except McKenna, who started to whine again about how she would surely fall off the branch and break her legs and arms. But again she resented and climbed up.

The next morning after everyone had awoken, Amethyst called them together and explained their plan.

When she was done, Josh and Emily tiptoed to a spot in the courtyard where they were best viewed from Mahalia's tower. Then Josh yelled, "Hey! You tried to trip me!" He tried to sound angry.

"Did not!" said Emily shakily. She normally was very shy so this was hard for her. But she knew she had to do it.

Her friends' lives depended on it.

"Did too," protested Josh.

"A-hem!" Mahalia's voice rang out, and Josh breathed a small sigh of relief. So far so good.

"What's going on down there?" demanded Mahalia angrily.

"Uh, nothing, Mal," said Emily loudly, trying to look mad.

"Nothing is incorrect!" blasted Mahalia. "And my name is Mahalia, or Queen Mahalia to you! And *WHAT ARE YOU DOING ON MY COURTYARD?*"

"May-girl is nobody worth answering," said Josh to Emily, trying to look angry also. "Why should we answer you anyway, you cutie cupcake?"

Mahalia flew into a rage. "I am not a cutie *nor* a cupcake! You'd better leave before I find my wand!"

Meanwhile, while Mahalia was distracted, Angelica and Amethyst were attempting to get inside the castle. They crept to the wall, and flattened themselves against it, out of Mahalia's view. McKenna and Courtney tiptoed around the castle to the back, where they planned to try the back door.

"You're just a bratty cute cupcake!" stormed Emily. "Give us fifty million reasons why we should listen to a bratty cute cupcake!"

"I'M NOT A BRATTY CUTE CUPCAKE!" screamed Mahalia, her face flushed with anger and her eyes piercing and red. "That's it, ugly kids! I'm coming down!"

Emily and Josh watched until they could see Mahalia's black hair bobbing down the stairs through a small window and then they took off until they got out of the courtyard.

Amethyst and Angelica took the opportunity and crept silently into the castle.

"Let's see if Mahalia has any maps posted on the walls," whispered Amethyst.

"Maps? In a castle?" Angelica looked aghast.

Amethyst shrugged silently. "Sure. This place's so big she'd get lost if she didn't."

Soon enough they did come across one. Amethyst traced her finger along it, mouthing the names of the rooms carefully, until she found Prisoners' Lair. According to this map, it was around the next corner, up the stairs, and around the corner.

She tiptoed to the corner and motioned for Angelica to follow. They had to be super-careful; Mahalia's slaves were normally everywhere, it was just lucky they had not ran into any yet. As they tiptoed towards the stairs, Angelica whispered, "I wonder how the others are doing."

Amethyst spotted a slave coming around the corner at the top of the stairs. "Ssh!" she hissed to Angelica and they ducked down on the stairs until the slave had left. Quickly, quietly, they ran around the corner.

Outside the castle, Josh and Emily were actually succeeding. In between yelling, "I'm in your courtyard!" and "Now I'm not!" they were screaming at Mahalia and calling her names. Mahalia was infuriated, and that was good. She needed to stay outside as long as possible so the others could perform their duties.

Angelica and Amethyst, inside the castle, finally made it to the Prisoners' Lair.

Amethyst tiptoed to the door and turned it carefully. As she had hoped, it was unlocked. So McKenna and Courtney had completed their duty.

But it had been barely five minutes. How could McKenna and Courtney find Eugenia and unlock the door in five minutes?

In a minute, she found out why.

Mahalia, despite what Steve had said, had practically no prisoners.

But the two she had besides Mary and Lucy made Amethyst gasp in shock.

They were Courtney and McKenna.

twenty-four
A Magic Ring

Immediately, McKenna tried to explain. "We were too loud, and-"

She was cut off by her captor, Eugenia, who was leaning from one foot to the other, arms folded, an evil smile on her face. She shot McKenna a hard look. McKenna silenced herself, and Eugenia turned her attention to Angelica and Amethyst.

"So, you've come to join your friends." She leaned forward to grab Amethyst, but Amethyst twisted out of the way. Angelica tackled Eugenia, and Amethyst attempted to jump on top of the villain, but Angelica stopped her.

"The rope!" she managed to yelp.

Amethyst, in understanding, grabbed the rope resting on a nearby hook. McKenna, Courtney, Mary, and Lucy were quick to jump up. Struggling, Eugenia fought her way to a sitting position.

McKenna spotted it, and let out a *whoop*. She jumped up and karate-kicked Eugenia in the face. Eugenia let out a groan and fell backwards. Mary and Amethyst, who had the rope, took the chance and began wrapping the rope around her, while Courtney and Angelica held her down.

"Wait, you don't want to do this!" Eugenia struggled for her wand but Angelica was quicker. She snatched the wand away.

"Amethyst?" she asked. "Now, I think, would be a good time to use that magic ring."

Amethyst turned towards Mary. "Mary, how do I work it?"

Mary struggled to remember. It was hard. She wasn't tied up or anything, but Eugenia had put a "zap border" around the room, and only the ring- *the ring which Amethyst now owned* - could release them. "Could I see it, Amethyst?"

Amethyst nodded and handed over the rubber band that Amethyst knew was going to somehow become the ring.

Mary took the rubber band from Amethyst. She put it over her finger, and held it up to the light. "Roses are red, violets are blue - turn into a ring, rubber band, I command you!"

Everyone gasped as ... nothing happened.

Eugenia laughed an evil laugh.

Mary worked for another half hour, trying to will the rubber band into a ring.

Eugenia continued to taunt them with laughter.

Finally, Amethyst asked quietly, "Mary, could I please try it?"

Mary willingly handed it over. "Sure."

Amethyst stared at the rubber band, trying to figure out its secret. Then it hit her. "Mary, what was that phrase you said early on, about sparkling stars or something?"

Mary's face lit up. "'Sparkle like a star and shine like a jewel,'" she said.

Amethyst held up the rubber band like Mary had done, and boldly said, "Sparkle like a star and shine like a jewel!"

Everyone held their breath ..... as again nothing happened.

Everyone was silent. Then Josh spoke up: "Amethyst, what if you tried snapping your fingers?"

Amethyst smiled. Once more, she held up the rubber band with her left hand, and said, "Sparkle like a star and shine like a jewel!" while snapping the fingers on her right hand.

Sparks flew, and the room was full with intense light as the rubber band leapt from her fingers onto the floor. A collective gasp filled the room as the light slowly faded and the ring came into view.

It was beautiful. Its sparkle was mesmerizing. It was filled with indescribable colors that none of them had ever seen before.

Eugenia was quiet. Terrified.

For the first time, McKenna was speechless. Courtney wanted to say 'wow' but was afraid McKenna would say it at the same time and jinx her - *again.*

They all stood and stared for a while until Amethyst slowly bent down, picked up the ring and slid it on her finger.

"Mary, what now?"

"All you have to do is make a wish. The person in possession of the ring controls it."

Amethyst looked confused.

"What's wrong, Amethyst?" Mary asked.

Amethyst thought for a moment, then said. "I can make a wish with a wand too. What makes this ring so special?"

"Think of it this way," said Mary. "The ring has seven million times more power than a wand. In other words, if you use the wand to wish us to escape, we can escape, but Mahalia can recapture us. If you use the ring when you wish it, Mahalia can never recapture us. And its magic never wears off. With wands, if you make, let's say, trees turn purple, you'd have to keep wishing it every year. It wouldn't last. But the ring's magic always lasts."

Angelica gawked.

Amethyst's mouth dropped open, too. "Amazing. No wonder the evil fairies wanted to get their hands on it. If they wish for us to be captured-"

Mary nodded. "That's right. But, there is one thing you need to know." Mary looked right into Amethyst's eyes, "Because of the ring's power, it must be used with caution. There are only so many wishes you can make."

"How many?" asked Angelica in interest.

"A lot," said Mary, "but still, there's a limited number of wishes, so we can't be using it to wish ridiculous things."

Amethyst nodded uncertainly. "I see."

"Now," Mary finished, "could you please wish us out of here?"

Amethyst nodded, and said loudly, "I wish Mary and Lucy -"

"Aren't you forgetting someone?" asked McKenna loudly.

Amethyst sighed. "I was getting to that. I wish Mary and Lucy, and McKenna and Courtney would be freed!"

Amethyst turned to Mary next. "Mary, can I just wish Miranda to be here, right now?"

Mary's face grew pale. "No, Amethyst, don't do that. If you do that, she could be.... hurt in the transferring because she is not free."

"I could-" started Amethyst.

"Honey cake." Mary placed a gentle hand on Amethyst's finger, which had the ring. "Trust me. We have to find her ourselves. And then we may use the ring."

Amethyst sulked. "Okay, let's go free up Josh and Emily. But first-" she shined the light at Eugenia. "I wish Eugenia would stay this way forever." Then she followed her friends out the door with Eugenia's screams and cries behind them.

Amethyst felt a tiny pang of sadness for the fairy, but Eugenia deserved it. She was more evil than any other person in the world.... well, maybe Mahalia was a bit more wicked.

They exited the castle. Mahalia swung around. "Yikes... Oh, Eugenia!" she called.

"Don't try to call," said Amethyst. She pulled out the ring. "I wish to defeat Mahalia."

Mahalia fell to the ground, wailing. "I'll get you back for this!"

Mary ignored her. "Troops, let's go."

"Go, go, go, go, go," sang McKenna as normal. "We've got the lead, lead-lead-lead! We're gonna win, win-win-win! The fairies are naughty, naughty-naughty-naughty! Now we're going, going-going-going!"

"Amethyst, wish to be back at your asylum," instructed Mary.

Amethyst hesitated. As much as she wanted to rescue Miranda, she couldn't bring herself to go back.

"Can you wish it?"

Mary said gently, "I can't, Amethyst, it doesn't really work for me. You can do it. For me. Do it for me."

Amethyst looked from the ring to Mary. She bit her lip and said, "I'll do it for you, Mary." Then she took a deep breath and said, "I wish to be back at Asylum Odelia."

chapter twenty-five
Back to Asylum
Odelia

Then they were swirling, and Amethyst felt like she had a headache, and that maybe she'd be sick. Her feet felt like they were bending the wrong way, and her eyes hurt to be opened. Her ears were popping and her body was flailing involuntary in ways it really wasn't supposed to be flailed.

In less than a minute, it was over, and they were standing outside the asylum Amethyst had left what seemed like so long ago.

Mary took a deep breath and entered. Amethyst's stomach dropped immensely and she felt rather sick when she saw Miss Odelia behind the desk.

Mary approached her. "Hello."

Miss Odelia looked up and sucked in her breath. "Well, hello." She spotted Amethyst. "I see, you found her on the streets and want to return her? I'll take care of it right away."

She grabbed Amethyst by the forearm and started to drag her

away. "You ever try to run away again, I'll have you *severely* punished."

"Wait!" Mary's voice called, much to Amethyst's relief. "That wasn't why I came here."

"Oh." Miss Odelia's cheeks flushed and she returned Amethyst. Amethyst rubbed her forearm. "What do you want, then?"

"I want to adopt a certain poor girl named Miranda," said Mary.

"Oh," said Miss Odelia smugly. "You're out of luck, then. We just shipped her off on the orphan train a few weeks ago." She smiled.

Amethyst's knees went weak.

"No," she whispered.

Mary searched for words. "Where did the train go?"

Miss Odelia said, "Its destination was the glamorous castle of Mahalia."

Amethyst frowned. She had just been there, and Miranda hadn't been there.

"Of course she's probably not there now. Mahalia does many things with the children we send her."

Mary's voice became very, very harsh. "Like what?"

Miss Odelia shrugged lazily. "Oh, I'm not sure. You'd have to ask her. She may have shipped her to another asylum. Or maybe she's still on the train."

Lucy tugged Mary's sleeve. "Mary, will we be able to find her?"

Mary nodded faintly. "I think so, love. Thank you, freaky lady, for your useless information," she hissed at Miss Odelia.

"Useless in-for-ma-tion," hissed McKenna, separating the syllables big time. She waved her hands to go with it. "Take that, you useless lady-lady."

Mary ushered them out, giving McKenna a stern look. As soon as they got outside, she frowned. "Amethyst, where's Emmy and Rachel?"

Amethyst's heart stopped for a second, and then she remembered. "At a doctor's office. We stopped at the Mochas' house for the night and the next day all they did was sleep, so we took them in."

"What was the doctor's office called?" Mary asked.

"Uh, I don't know, Dr. Sawyer's or something?" said Amethyst, shrugging. "Should we go get them?"

"No," said Mary, strangely very calm. "Wait here - I forgot to ask Miss Odelia something." She dashed back inside.

chapter twenty-six
Rebecca, Kayla, Delaney and Miranda

Hi. I'm Rebecca," said the dark figure.

Miranda's eyes were still not adjusted to the dark. "Hello. I'm Miranda."

"Sup girl," said another voice. "How's it goin' for you? The name's Delaney and I already like you!"

"Uh, thanks," said Miranda. "Anyone else here?"

"Yea," said a voice that sounded offended. "But I'm the last one. My name's Kayla. K-a-y-l-a. Kayla."

"Got it," said Miranda. She would've nodded if she could. "How long have you been here?"

"That's rude," Kayla commented. "But anyway, we've been here a week or two."

Miranda was horrified. "How do you survive?"

"Easy," said Delaney. "Listen to me. Nora unfreezes us every day to let us eat." She talked in a rap-like tone. Miranda liked it.

"Nora?"

"That lady who put you in here."

Miranda attempted to nod. "What do we eat?"

"Bread," responded Kayla. "B-r-e-a-d. Bread. And beans. B-e-a-n-s. Beans. And water. W-a-t-e-r. Water."

"Why are you spelling the things you say?" asked Miranda curiously.

"I don't want to forget how to spell," explained Kayla smugly. "Anyway... how'd you end up here?"

Miranda told her story from the beginning then, starting with arriving at her asylum when she was little, to her best friend Amethyst, to the terrors Emmy and Rachel; she told how depressed she was upon Amethyst's departure over a week ago, and up to the horrible day she was selected to ride.

When she was done, Rebecca tried to nod. "If you don't mind I'm not going to tell mine - "

" 'Cause I'm a-telling it for her! She arrived on July four!" sang Delaney.

Rebecca breathed a small sigh of relief. But before she could say anymore, the boxcar's door swung open and Nora stormed in angrily, holding four plates of beans and bread.

chapter twenty-seven
McKenna and a Bowl

Mary dashed back out. "We're not going anywhere, troops."

"Why?" asked McKenna in disbelief. "I was really looking forward to my hourly song! You've *got* to be kidding!"

"I'm not," said Mary plainly. "The next train's coming in this afternoon. We're staying and getting on."

Amethyst caught on. "That way, if Miranda's on the train still"-

"Exactly," said Mary, nodding. "If she's still on the train we'll be able to find her."

"Why can't - " Amethyst stopped. She had been about to ask 'why can't we wish to get her' but she then she had remembered Mary had said about it could hurt her to do that, so she stopped herself.

Mary gave her a look, obviously knowing what she had been about to say. "Anyone hungry?"

"Am I?" asked McKenna, again in disbelief. "You have to *ask* that? Seriously, Mary, you don't need to ask that question. Always assume it's a yes."

Mary bit back laughter. "I'll see to it, McKenna."

Amethyst frowned. She didn't understand. "Where will we get this food?"

Mary gestured to the asylum with a wide grin. "Here. Where else?"

Amethyst shook her head stubbornly. "Not here. All they feed you is slop." Well, they did serve soup once in a while, but mostly it was slop.

"They wouldn't dare feed guests slop," said Mary boldly and re-entered the asylum.

Miss Odelia narrowed her eyes. "What do you want now?"

Mary smiled slyly. "We've heard you have the best public restaurant and just simply had to try it out. Just I like I just said. You have a horrible memory."

Miss Odelia glared at Amethyst, obviously thinking it was her fault, even though it wasn't. "Of course. You just happen to come at eating hours. Would you care to eat with the other children?"

Mary looked at Amethyst with a questioning look.

Amethyst nodded. "We'll sit with the girls, please," Mary said.

"Excuse me for one moment," said Miss Odelia and rushed off in the direction of the cellar. Amethyst knew she was turning on the cafeteria's vents. It felt so.... well.... scary to be in the asylum again. Amethyst had to close her eyes most of the time, when Miss Odelia wasn't looking. She knew Mary would protect her, and they had the ring, but it was still awkward, weird, and frightening all at the same time to be back. She caught Angelica's glance. Clearly Angelica was remembering her old asylum, too.

Miss Odelia came back, full of false kindness. "Right this way, ladies and gents." She led them into the all-too-familiar cafeteria room. Amethyst swallowed, trying very hard not to be sick. She normally was fine with not getting sick; it was just something about returning that made her stomach ache.

Miss Odelia sat them in the middle of the room. Heads turned. Bodies swung. All cafeteria chat was silenced. All eyes were on the guests.

Amethyst swallowed again. She managed a look at the table

closest to her. There was soup in the bowl, not slop.

Miss Odelia clapped her hands. "Girls, what are you thinking, showing up in your ragged clothes when I told you this morning to dress nicely for our visitors? Are you trying to make this place look bad?"

"Excuse me," said McKenna loudly. "I'm afraid you are turning into a big fat liar, Miss Whatever-your-name-is. You didn't know we were coming for dinner until, oh, about five minutes ago, so you couldn't possibly had known this morning."

"You..." hissed Miss Odelia, then stood up straight and continued her fake kindness act. Her hands were clenched at her sides. All she said was then, "Someone else was supposed to come tonight but they cancelled. I didn't tell them because you showed up." Her voice was a monotone type of voice, her eyes on Mary and her body full of sharp points. Then she turned and stiffly walked to the buffet, gesturing for them to follow. "We have broccoli cheese soup tonight, and fresh bread."

Amethyst swallowed again.

Mary nodded and calmly spooned the chunky, thick soup into bowls. She handed them to everyone and sat down.

Amethyst tried to get an appetite. She sniffed the soup, trying to make herself smell it like it really was - delicious. She looked at it, trying to force herself to see it as it was - delicious. But even after she knew it was delicious, she couldn't bring herself to take even a spoonful of it. She had been hungry earlier, but now her appetite had completely disappeared. She swallowed yet again and quietly pushed the steaming soup away from her.

Around the table, everyone was enjoying it - pretty much.

McKenna was gulping down the soup as if her life depended on it, Courtney was eating quickly but still taking ladylike sips, unlike McKenna. Angelica was sipping it every so often and looking like she liked it. Emily was eating quietly and slowly, as if to savor each bite. Mary was stirring her soup and taking a small spoonful every so often. Lucy was taking big un-ladylike slurps like McKenna, except she was using her spoon. (McKenna was simply drinking the soup out of the bowl, and making quite a mess.) And Josh - Josh's soup was untouched, like Amethyst's. His bread had one bite taken out of it, and his water glass was empty, but otherwise his meal was not eaten.

Amethyst exchanged a glance with him. He looked at the soup and made a face.

Mary noticed. "Josh, Amethyst? What's wrong? Aren't you hungry?"

"No," said Amethyst in a tiny voice.

Crash! The crash of a bowl breaking silenced the whole cafeteria. Amethyst looked around and saw McKenna, now bowl-less, staring hard at Amethyst and Josh, her eyes moving quickly from one to the other. Her hands were still positioned to hold a bowl, except no bowl was there. She sat, un-moving.

Amethyst glanced under the table. There were parts of a bowl on the floor, surrounded by teeny tiny pieces, and on McKenna's lap was a rather big part of it.

"McKenna? What is the meaning of this?" Mary's voice became harsh. Amethyst tried to keep from laughing and her appetite began to return. She covered her mouth to muffle her giggles.

McKenna said nothing, did nothing, just kept staring at Amethyst. Amethyst began to laugh. She could see McKenna wanted to laugh also but was keeping still in order to make Amethyst laugh even harder, and that was just what Amethyst did.

"I will repeat myself," said Mary, her harsh voice now even harsher. Obviously she wanted a logical explanation from McKenna - an explanation she wasn't going to get - so she could avoid Miss Odelia's wrath. "What is the meaning of this?"

McKenna sadly relented. "Come on, Mary," she said sadly. "All I was trying to do is make everybody start laughing." She pouted.

Mary briskly stood up and gestured that they would go. Miss Odelia could get very crazy if she got mad and Mary didn't want that to happen. And so they trailed out of the asylum, followed by Miss Odelia's glare. *They would pay. They would all pay. And soon.*

* * * * * * * * * * * * * * * * * * * *

"We'll stay here until the train comes, then get on. Sound good?" asked Mary.

"No," said McKenna. "I felt as if I just cracked a bowl to smithereens on accident, and I don't want to face the owners of the bowl."

"I completely understand," said Courtney, nodding, "because you *did* just crack a bowl to smithereens."

McKenna made a face. "Oh."

Amethyst rolled her eyes. "Why'd you do that, anyhow, McKenna?"

McKenna shrugged. "I just wanted to make everyone start laughing so I could laugh with them and then say 'Jinx' and make Courtney owe me *another* soda. I guess I got a little carried away." She added sheepishly, "Sorry, Mary."

"It's all good," promised Mary. "Now everyone listen. Does anyone hear the train?"

Amethyst put her hands on her hips. "It's not coming, Mary, because Miss Odelia hasn't lined up the girls yet." She peaked through the asylum's glass doors to make sure she was right. She was. "When Miss Odelia lines them up the train's due to come soon."

Mary looked embarrassed. "You're right, honey cake. Well... who's interested in a game of Twenty Questions to pass the time?"

"Me!" McKenna practically screamed. "I'll go first." She scratched her head. "Hmm.. okay I've got a person. You'll never, *ever* guess who it is."

So they played for a while, and after they found out McKenna's person was - of all people - Courtney, they played again and found out Mary's person was Rachel, and kept playing until Amethyst heard the faint, shrill whistle of the orphan train.

She only looked at Mary, afraid if she opened her mouth she would be sick. Wasn't this the same place she had been so long ago? Why was she here again? Her breath came in short gasps, and the only comfort was that Mary was here, and they had the ring.

Mary pulled them over to the side as Miss Odelia shuffled more girls out the doors. She glared at them. "What are *you* doing *here?*" she growled.

"It's a free country," responded McKenna, "we have the right to go anywhere we like."

Miss Odelia eyed them. "Just don't get in the way of the train."

"Actually, Odelia," said Mary, "we were about to get on."

Miss Odelia flew into a mad rage, screaming in wrath.

"We heard," said Mary calmly, "how perfectly civil your train is, and we wanted to see for ourselves."

Miss Odelia shot Amethyst yet another glare, positive it was all her fault. "Well, come along, then," she said, just barely keeping her voice calm, and brought them onto the train ahead of all the others. "Pick your seats." Her voice became stiff.

Amethyst pointed out the worst seat on the train- the one with no window. She didn't want to look outside, and, besides, she wanted the poor children coming onto the train to have the best seats.

As the girls trickled on, Amethyst whispered to Mary, "If she's on here, she's in Boxcar 24."

Mary nodded. "We'll get there, don't you worry, Amethyst."

Amethyst hoped that was true.

chapter twenty-eight
Boxcar Thoughts

After they had eaten, and Nora had cleared their plates and left the dismal boxcar, Miranda attempted conversation.

"So? How's life going?" she joked.

"Can't you see?" asked Kayla. "It's not going well right now. Are you dumb or what?"

"Kayla, stop being mean," ordered Rebecca. "She's new here."

Miranda had a question. "Why are certain girls put aboard here?"

Delaney said, "Don't know, lady, don't know any more than you here know."

Miranda sighed. "I miss Amethyst."

"Amethyst?"

"My old friend from my asylum."

"Oh," said Delaney. "Was she nice? Did she rid your room of mice?"

"No," said Miranda. "That is, she was nice, but she didn't rid my room of mice. I miss her."

"You already said that," said Kayla. "Anyways, I understand, sort of. I used to know this girl named.... oh, I can't remember her name now. She wasn't my friend or anything, but I miss her scoldings so much."

"Scoldings?" Miranda was surprised.

Kayla smiled faintly. "Yeah, the scoldings. 'Kayla, stop making things up.' 'Kayla, I think my name means order.' I miss it all.. I just wish I could remember her name!"

Delaney sighed. "I'm officially bored. I wish I had a sword."

"What'd you do with a sword?" asked Rebecca, aghast.

"Break down the door, what do you think? And I definitely would not paint it pink!"

Miranda had a question. "Delaney- how do you always make things rhyme?"

"Easy," said Delaney, "I just do words that match up together. But sadly, I can't use the word begether."

Rebecca rolled her eyes. "You know, there's this rumor that another group of girls lived in this boxcar before us? Like, trapped like us?"

Miranda stared at her, amazed. "Really?"

"Yeah. I heard Nora talking about it. She said, 'This second group is much easier than Eugenia's first group.' Who do you suppose Eugenia is?" asked Rebecca dramatically.

"I don't know," said Miranda. "What.... what happened to the other girls?"

Rebecca shivered. "I really don't know. I don't even want to think about it. Nobody has said anything about what happened. " Rebecca was dramatic.

"Let's look on the bright side," said Delaney. "Maybe Miss Old Mean Nora lied."

Miranda attempted to shrug. "I hope you're right, Delaney."

chapter twenty-nine
Jump!

"Now's our chance, Mary. Let's go!" The coast was clear: all evil fairies were out of sight, and the conductor was on the phone.

Mary shook her head. "There's someone in the next coal car: I can just hear it. Someone bad."

Amethyst slumped in her seat. The train was rattling down the track at an amazing speed. The door connecting the passenger car with the coal car swung open, and a mirror-like image of Mahalia, except shorter, stepped out. She was holding four empty plates.

She saw Mary and hissed, "Get off my train, by order of Mahalia."

Mary rolled her eyes. "How many times do I have to tell you? It's a free country. I can ride any train I like."

"Not this one." The mirror-like image of Mahalia turned angry. "I bet none of your bratty children know my name. I just finished feeding some bratty girls in the boxcar and they barely remembered my name!"

Amethyst put on her I'm-so-innocent look and asked in a perfectly innocent voice, "Ma'am, why are there girls in the boxcar?"

"Shush up, girl," said the lady. "You know very well why- you were there yourself! Now be quiet and get off my train!"

Mary calmly got up, motioning for the others to follow. "If you need our spot we will stand."

"You will do no such thing!" the lady bellowed. She grabbed Angelica's wrist and began to drag her to the door. "I'll get you off this train if I have to do it myself!"

Amethyst lunged and grabbed Angelica, pulling her back. Startled, the lady let go. Angelica rubbed her wrist and hurriedly got to her feet. The lady rolled her eyes.

"Out - you can go yourselves the easy way, or I can do it the hard way!" She lunged forward again and grabbed Lucy. Lucy screamed, but she was no match for the lady - whoever she was. The lady dragged her to the door and threw her out.

Amethyst ran and jumped out afterword. She had already somewhat experience and landed gracefully. *Wow,* she thought. *When I was brought to the asylum I never thought I'd be jumping off orphan trains one day!*

"Lucy? You okay?" Amethyst helped the little girl sit up.

"Yea, I think," said Lucy.

Amethyst looked back and saw everyone had jumped off except McKenna. She was standing in the doorway with her hands over her eyes. "GO, GO, GO!" Amethyst screamed at her.

Another moment and she'd be too far away from them, and who knew what that lady would do then?

McKenna jumped, thankfully, and fell onto the grass face-first. Then she struggled up, rubbing her nose, and walked over to Mary.

Mary sighed. "Miranda was on that train, Amethyst."

Amethyst's head ached. They were so close, yet so far from her sister - her *twin* sister!

Mary continued, "She's close enough that if we use the ring to retrieve her, she'll be fine."

"We're in the middle of a big prairie," commented McKenna

suddenly, not matching the conversation topic at all. "Now, how did that happen?" she added, pretending to forget and drumming her fingers slowly on her chin, appearing to be in deep thought while she was really just trying to make everyone laugh. She succeeded. Everyone laughed.

Mary shot Amethyst a meaningful glance. Amethyst, with some delight, pulled the ring out of her pocket and caught the sun's rays on the surface of the ring. "I wish..."

Suddenly Angelica noticed the lady coming towards them. She had a wand in her hand and was pointing it at them.

"Amethyst! NO!" screamed Angelica, but it was too late. Just as the Ring completed Amethyst's wish, they were all spinning again. Amethyst was dizzy, and she got the feeling her knees were bending the wrong way again. When she opened her eyes she saw Mahalia's castle, the prairie, the train, and the asylum spinning and merging. Her eyes stung. Her head ached. Her stomach churned. And then it was over, and they were right in front of Dr. Sawyer's office.

* * * * * * * * * * * * * * * * * * *

Miranda was spinning. She was turning and twisting. Her head was hurting and she felt sick. *What was happening? Where am I? Where are Delaney, Rebecca, and Kayla?*

Then the spinning stopped. Miranda was alone in a prairie and felt dizzy. *Why was she alone in a prairie?*

She stood up carefully, and thought about what she did know. First, she was by the train tracks; second, it was warm out; third, she was perfectly alone; and fourth, she felt sick. Miranda shaded her eyes and looked around. The train tracks were there, of course, but besides that there was nothing in this bare land. She could follow the train tracks, but wherever the train headed was bad, someplace she didn't want to go.

Were her newfound friends alright? Had they been... *transferred* someplace alone, too? If not, were they alright?

Miranda's head swarmed with questions, and had nobody to answer them. Finally she decided her best bet would be to follow the tracks. *They must go through a town eventually.* Out loud she said, "I wonder how I got here."

She stood up and started following the tracks.

chapter thirty
Check-Up on the Twins

Oh no!" Mary groaned when she opened her eyes and saw they were not in a prairie, nor with Miranda. "Oh no!"

"Mary, look on the bright side," encouraged Emily. "We'll get to see Rachel and Emmy!"

Mary's angry look turned to one of surprise. "Really? They're here?"

"Yeah," said Courtney. "Come troops. And please don't sing, McKenna."

McKenna pouted but said nothing.

Mary took a deep breath. "I'll stay out here, to keep watch, with Lucy. You go on in, pick up the twins, and come right back out."

Amethyst nodded uncertainly. "Okay." She entered.

From the desk, Lexi looked up. "You again! How's the journey coming along?"

"Fine, thank you," said Angelica.

"We've come to check up on my sisters...." said Amethyst.

"Sisters? Oh, right," said Lexi. "Dad? The kids are back!"

Dr. Sawyer came out of the back room. "Oh, hello, kids. You've come about Miss Amethyst's sisters?"

Amethyst nodded carefully.

Dr. Sawyer motioned for them to sit down. "They're doing much better," he started. "They're awake and everything. But the persuasion part isn't cured yet- they still can be persuaded to do just about anything. I'm working on a cure, so they should be well again in a few weeks."

"Okay," was all Amethyst said.

"Can we see them?" asked McKenna.

Dr. Sawyer hesitated. He explained they shouldn't be seeing the twins because if they accidentally asked them to do anything they'd do it.

"So? We'll come back in a few weeks?" asked Courtney.

"Right-o, girl. Thanks for the check-up." Dr. Sawyer grinned.

Courtney grinned back shyly. "Thank you."

Dr. Sawyer smiled as he ushered them out. "Bye, kids."

"Bye, Dr. Sawyer," called McKenna. "Bye, Miss Clerk Lexi. Keep clerking for me!" and then Dr. Sawyer shut the door nicely.

Mary looked at them, puzzled. "Where's the twins?"

"Not better yet," said Josh. "They need a few more weeks."

Amethyst saw Mary's look and explained the whole disease they seemed to have. Mary nodded.

"Let's go search," said Amethyst. "If I can't have Rachel and Emmy, I want Miranda." Silently, she added, *And if I can't have Miranda, get me my fourth sister who you will say nothing about.*

Mary laughed. "Don't be so demanding, honey cake. Let's try to find our way back to that prairie."

"No," said Emily quietly. "It'll take us weeks and days to get back there, and Miranda will most likely not be there once we get there."

Mary considered. Emily had a point. "You're right, honey. The thing is, what else can we do?"

Amethyst disagreed with Emily. "Mary, you said the ring had powers beyond wands. If I wished Miranda to be there, she can't

140

leave the prairie because of magic!"

Mary said, "No, honey cake. The way the wish works is so she could move other places."

"That makes it harder," said Angelica. "Can't you just wish us to be there - wherever she is?"

Mary hesitated. "It'd hurt a lot more in the process."

"No thank you," said Amethyst quickly. "Thanks, but no thanks. I'd prefer finding her on *foot*."

"You can say that again," said Courtney. "Every time we use magic to get places I get headaches, stomachaches, dizziness, stinging..."

Amethyst nodded in understanding. "You guys go ahead and use magic, we'll use walking."

"No," said Mary. "We're going together. Got that? Together. If we decide to use magic, we're all using magic. Got it?"

"No," said Amethyst and Courtney in unison. "We'll walk."

Mary sighed. "Let's go find someplace to eat. I have a few dollars in my pocket, maybe enough to have a good meal at a restaurant."

chapter thirty-one
Goodnight!

What in the whole world just happened?" Kayla asked, trying to rub her eyes for the five millionth time.

"Miranda disappeared, that's what happened," said Rebecca as if disappearing was the most common thing in the world.

"This stuff is driving me crazy! I think I'm becoming lazy!" groaned Delaney. "She was here - I'm getting fear!"

"The question is, how did it happen?" asked Rebecca, frowning. "I mean, as far as I know, magic doesn't exist -"

"As far as you know," said Kayla. "Perhaps it does."

Rebecca waved it away. "Impossible."

"We're frozen," pointed out Delaney, "and magic causes freezin'."

Kayla looked at Rebecca. "Delaney's right. Only magic could cause us to be frozen."

Rebecca still was doubtful. "Maybe she's making us think we're frozen, when we're really not."

Delaney stared at Rebecca. "Nora's to blame, she had a wand when she came."

Rebecca pointed out it looked like a stick.

"Sticks don't freeze the breeze," protested Delaney, "but wands can with help from man."

Rebecca gave up. "Okay, maybe it does exist. Anyhow, we're not going to fight about it any longer."

* * * * * * * * * * * * * * * * * *

Amethyst sat in a comfortable booth in a warm, good-smelling restaurant. On one side of her sat Emily, and on the other McKenna. Next to McKenna was Angelica and Mary sat on the other side with Courtney, Josh and Lucy

The waitress came with their food. "Chicken and potatoes?" Amethyst took the meal and dug in. The mashed potatoes were creamy, buttery, and salty, the way she liked it, and the fried chicken was greasy and warm. Her side, french fries, were crispy and hot, slathered with cool ketchup. Her first soda ever, Sprite, tasted better than anything she had ever had before, and within a minute it was gone. Mary laughed and ordered another one.

McKenna was sipping her Sprite and glaring at Courtney. "Now you know what soda tastes like," she glowered. "*Now* you can buy me twenty-seven million sodas."

Courtney said, "Whatever," and sipped her root beer. "You'd get sick if you ate that many -"

"Sodas!" chimed in McKenna. "Ha! Now you owe me *twenty-eight* million sodas!"

Courtney responded with her usual 'whatever' and took a bite of her turkey.

When they were all done eating Mary ordered chocolate milk and ice-cream sundaes for all of them. Amethyst, who had barely ever had ice cream before, was very grateful and took as tiny bites as possible, wanting to make it last.

When they were finally done eating, Mary paid the bill and they left, full and content. When they got out, Mary said, "Everyone full?"

"Yes," they chorused, only this time it didn't end with McKenna's normal 'you owe me a soda'.

Mary sighed then, sadly. "We'll have to get directions tomorrow to the asylum." She glanced at the darkening sky.

"So much has happened today," said Angelica sadly. "It's been such a long day. We rescued Mary and Lucy, we defeated Mahalia and Eugenia, we started our search for Miranda...."

"Sure has been a long day," agreed Mary. "You guys must've woken up really early - when you arrived at the castle, it was only eight-thirty."

"So -" said Amethyst, " - we arrived at the asylum around one o'clock!"

"Exactly - and now we need to sleep," scolded Mary gently.

Amethyst frowned, not understanding how they could sleep in front of a busy restaurant.

Mary saw her look and laughed. "Silly girl, Amethyst! There's a hotel down the way - I saw it a few months ago when I was traveling through town."

"Oh. Phew," said Amethyst, relieved not to have to sleep in a tree or on hard ground.

Courtney frowned. "Won't it be expensive to sleep in a hotel, instead of your house?"

Mary ruffled Courtney's hair. "Silly, my house is miles away. We're in a city called - I believe - Donut, and I live in Glazings."

McKenna giggled. "Donut - a city named Donut! Are they famous for their donuts or something?"

Mary laughed, too, and explained that it was simply a name they chose. "The founder's last name was Donut, so that's what they named it," she ended.

McKenna nodded. "I see now."

Mary led the way down narrow streets to a hotel. After they were all settled in the comfortable beds, and before they fell asleep, Mary flicked on the lamp and began to quietly explain the next day's plan. She explained they'd find their way to the asylum and go from there. Then she turned off the light.

Right before she fell asleep, Amethyst pulled the ring out of her pocket and gazed into its endless depths. It was a sapphire.

Still not an amethyst. Amethyst sighed, closed her eyes, and fell into a deep, dreamless sleep.

* * * * * * * * * * * * * * * * * * *

Miranda felt dizzy again, although this time it wasn't from being whisked away somewhere and abandoned, it was from walking in circles all day. At least it felt that way. Miranda had been walking for what seemed like an eternity and it felt like she was just going in circles. She was so hungry she probably could be going in circles and she wouldn't notice it. Finally she stopped walking and lay down, breathing hard. She looked up to see if anything was ahead of her, but her eyes crossed and she couldn't see anything. She closed her eyes and lay face-down. At least she wasn't frozen anymore, but her mouth was dry and her stomach growled. She was too dizzy to walk anymore, so, not knowing what else to do, she fell asleep.

A while later she was woken by someone rubbing her back. She opened her eyes and turned over. A teenage girl, probably seventeen or eighteen, stood over her. Miranda stared.

The girl looked on kindly. "Are you okay, little one?"

Miranda said, "I'm hungry... and thirsty.... and dizzy..."

The girl picked Miranda up and began carrying her. The sway from the walking felt soothing and in a minute Miranda was asleep once more, so she didn't see it when the girl carried her into a large city called Donut and brought her straight into Dr. Sawyer's office.

chapter thirty-two
Time to Get Moving

Wake up, girl. Wake up, get up, wake up, get up, GET UP!"

Without even opening her eyes Amethyst knew who was talking. She turned over. "I'm still sleeping."

McKenna gave her a look, even though Amethyst couldn't see. "It's time to get up. Mary said so."

Amethyst groaned and rolled over to glance at the clock. 8:56.

"Okay, I'm up, I'm up," she said, getting out of bed. Everyone else was already up and dressed.

Mary opened the door. "We'll catch some breakfast and then be out, okay, gang?"

Amethyst nodded, and followed Mary down the stairs to a nice hotel lobby. The lobby had tables and chairs, and in one section, waffle makers. There were donuts and muffins.

Amethyst selected two chocolate donuts, one blueberry muffin, made a waffle, and then sat down. As she took up her water-glass to take a drink, somebody bumped her arm. The water sloshed out of the glass and all over the table, floor, and Amethyst.

The person said, "Oops, sorry," then disappeared up the stairs before Amethyst could see who it was.

A hotel assistant rushed over with paper napkins. "I'm so sorry," the assistant apologized, cleaning up the water. "I'm sorry, but you'll have to move to a different table while I clean up this mess."

Amethyst didn't hesitate. After doing her best to dry her dress, she moved to the table on her right, where Angelica and Emily were sitting, and began to silently eat her muffin.

Mary moved, too. Amethyst looked at her. "Who was that?"

McKenna, from the other table, rolled her eyes. "Duh. A weirdo."

Mary ignored McKenna. "I'm... not quite sure, honey cake."

Amethyst knew Mary was lying. "Mary."

"Okay. I think it was -" Mary leaned in closely. "Odelia." Amethyst clapped hand to her mouth to stifle her gasp. "No! Not Miss Odelia!"

"I'm afraid so," whispered Mary. "Remember the unpleasantness at the asylum? And the train stuff? She's onto us."

Amethyst groaned inwardly. She took a bite of the donut, but it tasted flavorless in her mouth.

* * * * * * * * * * * * * * * * * * *

After breakfast, Mary signed out of the hotel and led them out. "Remember today's plan, anybody? We're headed to the asylum."

Amethyst, once more, groaned. She felt sick at the fact she was going there *again*.

Mary sensed her annoyance. "If you don't want to rescue your sister -"

"No!" Amethyst practically yelled. "I do! I just don't want to go back there!" She didn't have to say what 'there' was. Mary already knew.

"Honey cake -" started Mary.

"I know, I know," sighed Amethyst. "It's the only way we have a chance of finding Miranda, and okay, I'll go. I just don't want to."

Mary seemed satisfied. They began to walk down the busy road until they came upon an old man walking a collie dog. Thankfully, he was kind, even though a bit gruff, and gave Mary a map of the area. Mary thanked him, and they hurried away.

Mary looked at the map. "Amethyst, what street are we on, honey cake?"

Amethyst looked around carefully for the street sign, but all she saw was rustling bustling people around every corner. Finally, she spotted a small green sign at one corner. She strained to read it, but somebody was blocking her view. "I don't know, someone's blocking my view," she told Mary.

Mary glanced up. "Just wait for her or him to move."

Amethyst did. She looked at the person, tapped her foot, and looked at the person. She tapped her foot again impatiently.

Mary rolled her eyes. "I see you are impatient, Amethyst. Well, go ahead, ask her or him to move it."

Amethyst felt uneasy. She didn't like the idea of marching up to a stranger and telling it to "move it." Mary saw her uneasiness and asked if anyone else wanted to do it.

McKenna volunteered right away. "I'm not scared of some dumb old stranger," she said, and marched right up to the stranger.

Amethyst still felt uneasy. "Mary? Could we -" She stopped mid-sentence and stood dead silent, her eyes fixed on the stranger which McKenna was now approaching. The stranger had turned, revealing her face.

Mary turned towards Amethyst. "What -" She stopped, too, seeing the stranger. Even McKenna noticed and backed away, her eyes wide. Nobody said anything or did anything. They just stared at the person who they thought they had rid themselves of.

chapter thirty-three
Two Reappearances

Queen Mahalia advanced on them slowly, grinning evilly.

Finally Amethyst said, "We defeated you." She said it flatly, in disbelief.

Mahalia stopped. She considered. "Yes, that's true."

Amethyst turned to Mary. "Mary?"

Mary said, "Amethyst, she's defeated, powerless. But that doesn't mean she's dead. She cannot take us prisoner, but she can walk and talk and stuff."

"That's right," said Mahalia, cackling wickedly. "So come with me, folks."

Mary sighed loudly. "No thanks." To the group, she added, "Come on, kids, let's go." They turned away at Mary's command and began to walk away.

"Hey, wait up!" called a voice. "It's not over yet!"

Surprised, Amethyst looked behind her - and saw Mr. Chuckchester, coming up behind Mahalia!

Mary noticed. Her mouth fell open.

Mr. Chuckchester gave a salute. "Nice to see you again. Now..." He grabbed Mahalia's arm and dragged her into a small alley by them, despite Mahalia's screams.

A minute later he emerged Mahalia-less.

Mary gawked. "Did you...."

"Don't mention it," he said. Giving another salute, he began to walk off.

"Wait!" cried McKenna. "I don't understand. What did he do, Mary?"

Mary smiled. "Just think of it this way, Kenna: Thanks to him, we now no longer have to worry about Mahalia. She's gone for good."

"Oh," said McKenna dramatically. "Oooooh. I see, Mary. Oh, and my name is McKenna."

* * * * * * * * * * * * * * * * * * *

Rebecca had decided Miranda was gone, for good.

"Perhaps she was just a figment of our imagination," suggested Kayla.

"Lies," argued Delaney. "You're making up lies, because I saw her with my very own eyes. She's not pretend, because I saw her bend."

"When?" demanded Rebecca.

Delaney shrugged. "I didn't see her bend. Just bend rhymes with pretend."

"From now on," said Kayla, "please speak things that are true."

Delaney nodded. "You can trust me, because I would love to climb a tree."

Rebecca rolled her eyes, exasperated. "Next subject, guys. Should we attempt escape, or not?"

"No," said Delaney, "listen to me. Miranda'll rescue us, you'll soon see. She knew us, so she'll get a bus. She'll help soon, by the light of the moon." She thought, and then added: "Or by the sun, while eating a bun." She stopped, seeing Kayla's face. "Maybe not a bun, but maybe in the sun. Besides, she'll bring us food, that'll make me in a better mood."

Kayla looked at Rebecca in confusion.

Rebecca explained, "Delaney only sings her words to pass the time. If she were in a happy mood she'd talk."

"No," said Delaney, "I'm not eating no bun. I only sing cause it's really, really fun. I'll keep singing after Miranda comes, even if I'm doing plain old boring sums."

Kayla sighed with Rebecca. "You know what? I actually miss Miranda. She was really nice."

"Exactly," said Delaney. "I think so too. That's why she'll rescue us if it's the last thing she'll do."

* * * * * * * * * * * * * * * * * *

Miranda woke in a comfy bed with a pillow under her head and blankets piled on top of her. Sitting up, she realized she was very weak, and fell back down. As she did, she realized she was wearing very comfortable pajamas. For a minute she didn't know anything, but then it came back. Who was the kind teenage girl, and where was she now?

At that moment, the teenager came into the room. "Oh, I'm glad you're awake!" she cried, and called, "Dad, the girl's up!" Then she came into the room. "Are you okay? Need anything?"

"Breakfast?" asked Miranda.

"Of course, honey. What would you like?" The teenager got up from the bed.

"Whatever.... just something." Miranda closed her eyes. The girl nodded and exited the room. It was so silent, so dimly lit, so comfortable, Miranda wanted to fall back asleep. But soon the smell of bacon roused her. *Bacon.* She had never eaten such a delicacy, but had heard of it.

The girl came back into the room with a plate of scrambled eggs, bacon, and toast on a tray. She opened the window blinds and helped Miranda to sit up by propping pillows up behind her. Miranda ate slowly, to make it last.

The girl laughed. "You can have seconds. And thirds, too."

Miranda blushed.

"By the way," said the girl, sitting on the bed, "my name's Lexi. What's yours?"

"Miranda," said Miranda cautiously. "I'm not sure of my last name."

"That's fine," said Lexi. "My last name's Danalla."

"LEXI!" thundered a masculine voice from the opposite side of the office. "Lexi Smumble!"

Lexi blushed. "Uh, sorry. To protect me, my dad had us... uh... make up new last names. I keep forgetting."

"It's fine....?" said Miranda, with a question mark. She finished her eggs, asked for more, and ate them too. After she had finished, Lexi cleared her plate, and then her dad came in.

He extended his hand, and Miranda shook it. "Dr. Sawyer at your service," he said. "I see my daughter-clerk, Lexi, has gotten you food. I assume you are feeling better, Miranda?"

Miranda eyed him. How did he know her name?

"In case you're wondering Lexi told me your name."

Oh. Miranda relaxed. "Thank you for your hospitality." She hesitated. "How.... how... how many other patients do you have?"

"Two," said Lexi for her father. "Two four-year-old twins. Girls. Why do you wanna know?"

"I just...." Miranda shrugged. Why she really did it was because she had been hoping by some miracle Amethyst was here, or at least someone she knew. Wait - she used to know two four-year-old girl twins! Trembling, she asked, "What - what are their names?"

"Emmy and Rachel, I believe," said Dr. Sawyer, and Miranda fell back.

Not only was she alone, abandoned, and tired, she was stuck in the doctor's office with only the two terrible monsters.

chapter thirty-four
At Dr. Sawyer's

They aren't that bad," said Lexi to Miranda. "Actually, they're the sweetest little girls I've ever met. When you get strong enough I can take you to see them."

Miranda was still not sure. "I don't know. I remember them as troublemakers."

"All they do now is cry for their sister. That's not very trouble-ish, or something a troublemaker would do, is it?"

Miranda had to admit it wasn't. "What is their sister's name?" She hadn't known Emmy and Rachel had a sister.

"Amethyst, but I'm not sure. Whoever she was, she dropped them off herself. She was really worried about them, along with the bunch of kids she had with her."

"Amethyst?" breathed Miranda. She hadn't know Amethyst was the troublemakers' *sister!* Why had Amethyst never told her?

"She stopped by recently," said Lexi, "a couple days ago, before you came. Was in the area, wanted to check in on them. Since they weren't better yet, my dad told them to come back in a few weeks, so they'll probably be here in the next week or so. But maybe not, they're on a journey in the midst of all this."

A journey? For what? Miranda suddenly had a thought. *A journey to find* her?

"Hungry?" Lexi interrupted her thoughts. "It's past noon already. Do you want a turkey sandwich or soup?"

"Sandwich, please," said Miranda politely. She had had enough bad experiences with soup at the asylum. "And could I have chips for a side?"

Lexi smiled kindly. "Of course, dear." She left the room, and Miranda thought. Amethyst had been here, no doubt, and she was most likely coming back. If she could stay here until Amethyst returned, she could see her old friend again. But if she got better before Amethyst came.... well, she wasn't sure Dr. Sawyer would let a healed patient stay at his office. Sure, he let Lexi, but Lexi was his *daughter*, and Miranda wasn't.

Miranda decided she'd deal with that problem when the time came.

chapter thirty-five
For All We Know

In the boxcar, Kayla and Rebecca were once more doubting Delaney's predictions.

"Stop your doubt," said Delaney. "and please don't pout. She liked us, didn't she? So she'll help us, you just wait and see."

Rebecca frowned. "I'm not sure she liked us."

Kayla agreed. "Didn't seem too enthusiastic."

"But, she knew us," argued Delaney. "I'll bet she'll catch a bus.

She knew our troubles, so she'll rescue us before she even blows bubbles."

"I bet she doesn't even *have* bubbles," muttered Kayla.

Rebecca told Kayla not to be rude. "I wasn't being rude," argued Kayla.

"Where is she, you wonder?" asked Rebecca. "For all we know, she's trapped in another boxcar, on another train, in another state."

Nobody had anything to say to that.

* * * * * * * * * * * * * * * * * * *

"Feeling better today?" Lexi came into Miranda's room in the morning with a breakfast tray of pancakes. Miranda had been in bed ever since she arrived, and was eager to get out, but she still felt weak. She was stronger, and felt less tired, but she still didn't feel too well.

"A little," Miranda admitted, eating the pancakes. Lexi laughed. "Your appetite is definitely improving!"

Miranda blushed and drank her juice. "Could I have some more?"

Lexi laughed again. "Certainly." She disappeared out of the room and came back a minute later with another tray of food.

While Miranda ate, Lexi sat on the bed.

"My dad and I," she started, "were thinking today would be a good day for you to see Emmy and Rachel. My dad thinks you're strong enough, and the twins are just about better. They just need a week's worth of daily medicine, and they'll be better. Why, just last night, they were jumping on the bed!"

Miranda froze. See the troublemakers?

Lexi smiled gently. "We'll go as soon as you're done eating. I'll let you alone for a bit. When you're done call me and we'll go." Lexi left the room.

Miranda ate the rest of her breakfast slowly. There was no flavor in the food. She really did not want to see the twins, but she didn't want to insult Lexi.

When Lexi came back, she helped Miranda carefully out of bed. She carefully put her weight on one foot, then the other. She was stronger than she thought. With Lexi helping, Miranda walked out of the room and across the lobby. Dr. Sawyer was already there. "How are you doing?"

"Good, sir," said Miranda politely.

Dr. Sawyer said, "Excuse me for one minute," and disappeared into the room. Miranda heard him say "Girls, you have a visitor."

The all-too-recognizable voices of Rachel and Emmy made Miranda shiver. "Is it Amethyst?"

"No, sweetie." Dr. Sawyer exited the room. "Are you ready?"

Miranda nodded. She was as ready as she'd ever be. So she entered the room.

chapter thirty-six
Miranda is Reunited with the Twins

Rebecca decided they should forget Miranda.

"It's causing too much trouble," she explained.

Delaney didn't think so. "I'll never forget that girl. She'd stick with us through a windstorm whirl."

"Maybe not," said Kayla.

"She'd do it. You'll see when she comes back." Delaney was serious enough that she didn't speak in rhyme, so Kayla and Rebecca believed her, and that was the end of that.

* * * * * * * * * * * * * * * * * *

"Who're you?" demanded Rachel the minute Miranda walked

in. She was standing on the rumpled bed, arms crossed. "You're not big sissy."

"Of course I'm not," said Miranda faintly. "I'm Miranda."

Emmy studied her. "Oh, I know you!" She leaped out of bed and wrapped her tiny arms around her. "I missed you! And you know what? Big sissy misses you too! She said she was going to find you! I heard her when I was sleeping!"

"So did I!" proclaimed Rachel. "She said she'd rescue you! And we were too! But then we fell asleep!"

Emmy gaped. "Hey! Rachel! We did rescue her! She's here! Wait until Big Sissy sees this!"

Miranda could not believe her eyes. She had remembered Rachel and Emmy as terrible monsters, and now they were only sweet little figures!

Miranda turned to Dr. Sawyer. "What's wrong with them?"

"They had a rare disease," said Dr. Sawyer. "They could be persuaded to do anything at all. They're just about cured, we're just waiting to see if the medicine did its job. I can't send them away, though, because their sister hasn't returned yet and I can't seem to locate the person they said to leave them with...." He stopped, puzzled. "It seems to be she's nowhere in the area."

Miranda shrugged. "That is puzzling, but there's most likely a logical explanation. Maybe the person is on vacation or whatever."

Rachel interrupted. "What person name? 'Cause if her's name's Pacific I bet she on vacation in Pacific Ocean!" She exploded with laughter.

"Uh," said the doctor. He left the room and Miranda followed. At the desk Dr. Sawyer shuffled through some papers.

"Ah, yes, Mary Littles."

"Mary! She's here?" asked Emmy, rushing up behind Miranda and grabbing her legs.

Aghast, Dr. Sawyer looked at his little patient. "You *know* her?"

"*Know* her?" Rachel sounded like an adult. "She's our......
our.. l..leader. She helps! She helped Big Sissy!"

Dr. Sawyer backed up a bit. "Wait a minute. Why wasn't she

here when your big sister dropped you off?"

Emmy thought. "Hm. Oh I know! I know!"

"No, I know! Let *me* tell him!" said Rachel.

"No, *I* want to tell him!" yelled Emmy.

"Girls, girls," said Dr. Sawyer. "Rachel, you tell."

Emmy pouted.

"And Emmy, you will be my Special Personal Helper. You will fill in any details Rachel forgets, *after* Rachel has finished."

Emmy grinned broadly.

Rachel began. "She was captured!"

* * * * * * * * * * * * * * * * * * * *

After they had settled down under a tall tree to sleep, Amethyst and Mary were the last to fall asleep. Amethyst decided to try to explain her feelings to Mary: as much as she wanted to find Miranda, she wanted this all to be over.

"Mary?" she whispered, rolling over and touching their leader's back.

"Yes, honey cake?" Mary turned over.

"Mary.... I really want to find Miranda."

Mary looked at her. "I know, Amethyst."

"Yes...." Amethyst searched for words. "But on the same note.... I want this— this adventure to be over."

Mary studied her.

"I want my mother. I have no idea who she is, but still....." Amethyst sighed. "I want a real family."

Mary seemed surprised. "I understand, Amethyst." She paused. "Maybe someday, darling, maybe someday."

Amethyst rolled over again. She stared out at the stars. Maybe somewhere out there Miranda was staring up at the stars too. Amethyst kept her eyes on the nighttime sky until finally, she fell asleep.

* * * * * * * * * * * * * * * * * * *

All of a sudden Miranda remembered her past. Not her past-past, like asylum and stuff, she already knew that. And it wasn't like she didn't know and now knew. She had known the whole time, but just suddenly it had clicked in her brain.

Delaney.

Rebecca.

Kayla.

Miranda was lying in bed when she remembered, after a successful, even happy trip to Emmy and Rachel's room. She wanted, *needed*, to call Lexi, but it wasn't mealtime, and if she hollered Lexi'd think something horribly awful had happened, when it hadn't. And of course Miranda didn't feel strong enough to get up and walk. So she lay there impatiently, fidgeting and tossing, until finally Lexi came in.

"My goodness, Mir-mir, you're sure anxious!" she commented, sitting down on the bed. "What's a-happenin?"

Miranda explained best she could. "Please, *please* help them," she pleaded.

Lexi was baffled. "How?"

Miranda fell back in her bed. "I don't care. Just do it."

Lexi blinked. "You want me to invade a moving train to rescue three helpless girls trapped by the magic of somebody really evil."

Miranda breathed a sigh of relief that Lexi had gotten it. "Yup. I'll help, too, once I feel stronger."

Lexi nodded. She got up and exited the room hazily.

chapter thirty-seven
Nora! Oh No!

In the morning, they were woken by a trumpet. Amethyst
sat up. McKenna sat up. Courtney sat up. One by one, they all sat
up, rubbed their eyes, and stared at the green figure in front of
them.

"Mr. Chuckchester?" gasped Amethyst.

The figure whisked off her hat. "Guess again! And you'll
never, ever, ever guess, ever in a million trillion years!" Her voice
had a definite evil edge to it, but it was an unfamiliar voice.

Mahalia? No. Eugenia? Definitely not. Miss Odelia? Nope.
Miss Quiana? No way.

"Declare yourself," demanded Mary.

The figure took off her mask and her green coat, which had
made her appear green. Underneath was an unfamiliar face that
looked somewhat like Mahalia's. She had black hair like chopped
short at her shoulders. It had streaks of red in it, and she wore
white diamond-covered glasses. Her ears had no earrings. She was
wearing a short red dress with pink nylon tights and red shoes.
Her arms clanked with each movement courtesy of the millions of
red bracelets she wore. Her nails were bright red. Since her eyes

were hidden behind large black shades, Amethyst had no idea what color her eyes were, but she suspected red. She had black lipstick, too, coating her lips.

"Bow to your princess," demanded the green figure. "I'm Queen Mahalia's - excuse me, *was* Queen Mahalia's daughter, Princess Nora. I now live with my father. I like him a lot more than my wonderfully wicked mother, who was unfortunate enough to be dead right now." Her voice had a hint of sarcasm, and she strolled around them as she said it. "What a pity. I am now taking over her job."

McKenna said, "Don't you dare try to trick us into thinking you're Mahalia's daughter. Nobody ever said she had a daughter - or a husband!"

"Exactly," said Nora. "We were hiding, so when the time came that my mother died, we could come out and take the world by surprise." This daughter of Mahalia's was obviously five times as evil as her mother. "In fact, I am now Queen Nora."

Amethyst was in shock. Mahalia had a daughter - and a husband?

Nora continued, "Anyhow, my father wanted to keep going on my mother's mission, so he sent me out here to take you by surprise and capture you." She reached out to grab Amethyst, but Amethyst regained sense and jumped out the way. She got into a karate pose, even though she knew it would do no good. Like she thought, when Nora saw her, she laughed.

Amethyst felt her face heat up. She did not want to go through with being captured again; she wasn't sure if Mr. Chuckchester could help them again a second time.

So, even though she knew she was facing a fairy - or at least a half-fairy - she flew at Nora with her fists.

Nora seemed surprised but seemed not hurt in the least. In a quick motion, she swept Amethyst to the floor. "How cute. The little girl wants to defend herself." Nora leaned down and picked Amethyst up gingerly. She held her in one hand while bending down to speak into her watch. "Queen Nora to castle, Queen Nora to castle, I need backup. Repeat, I need backup. Over." She turned to the squirming Amethyst and rolled her eyes.

Mary's hand went to her pocket. Her fingers searched but pulled out nothing. Amethyst began to panic, and assured herself Mary was just tricking Nora.

Then suddenly she had a hope.

She leaned towards Nora's frilly black hair. She winced, closed her eyes, and drove her fingers into Nora's messy hair. Nora hissed in surprise and began fighting, as if she knew what Amethyst had in mind.

With her fingers still embedded in the evil fairy's hair, Amethyst snapped them. Like she thought, instead of a spark flying upwards, the hair blocked it and a strand of black hair caught on fire, quickly spreading to the other hairs.

Nora screamed and dropped Amethyst, who pulled her fingers free of loose hairs and scampered to Mary, who held her tightly.

"Magnificent job, honey cake," she whispered. Then she said, "Does anyone see the backup Nora called?" She glanced at Nora, who was a ways away, jumping and shrieking and grabbing at her burning hair which had spread to her dress.

Nobody did.

Soon, however, McKenna started yelling, "Bad fairies coming from the east! Repeat, fairies from the east!" She was jumping up wildly and pointing behind Amethyst. She turned, seeing Miss Quiana and Miss Odelia advancing.

Emily snapped her fingers, and a spark drifted out. "Just testing."

Mary had them all test their sparking abilities. Amethyst wondered why she could do that. Regular human beings couldn't make sparks from snapping fingers. So why could she?

Amethyst remembered that she could jump high and walk lightly and told the others to remember. Then Miss Odelia came forward, glaring. "How dare you," she said, seeing Nora screeching her head off around the corner, and reached to grab Amethyst.

Amethyst was prepared. She jumped, and Miss Odelia's hands closed on nothing. Amethyst flew over Miss Odelia's head and landed gracefully behind her. Miss Odelia swerved, and Amethyst jumped again, this time landing on Miss Odelia's head, planning to light her hair on fire also. But Miss Odelia somehow knew her tricks and reached up, taking hold of her by her arms.

With her last bit of freeness, Amethyst bent down to Miss Odelia's head and snapped her fingers. But her hands were too high and the spark floated harmlessly into the air. Gasping, she struggled and tried to jump, but Miss Odelia's grip was too firm. Miss Odelia placed her on the ground and pulled her, forcing her to walk, and it was then she remembered her walking. She began to walk fast and she had so much force and belief she bounded off the ground and over Miss Odelia. Then her feet touched down and then she was bounding through the air once more.

Surprised, Miss Odelia found her arm going in circles, and she yelped and let go. Amethyst took the chance and snapped. Her timing was perfect and in a second Miss Odelia was screaming her head off along with Nora and Miss Quiana.

"It was easy to get Quiana," commented Josh. "All I had to do was show her my fists and she screamed like a baby, which gave Emily the perfect chance to snap her fingers."

After the screaming fairies had left their sight, Mary gathered them close and put Amethyst in charge. "Lead us to Miranda, Captain Amethyst!" she declared.

Amethyst's cheeks flushed. "Uh, thanks, Mary." She really had no idea where Miranda was; she just felt she was in the area. Where should she look first? Well, Dr. Sawyer's office was around here. They could check up on the twins, and then if they were better, they could take them with on the continuing journey. Yes, that would do. "Let's check up on the twins first. Is that okay, Mary?"

Mary nodded, looking dreamy. "Do you know where it is?" Amethyst frowned. She searched her memory. Dr. Sawyer's office was by Mrs. Mia's house. Mrs. Mia's house was in the neighborhood ahead of her. That meant..... "Yes, I know where it is," she told Mary, and carefully led them straight to Dr. Sawyer's office.

chapter thirty-eight
Family Gathering

The first thing Amethyst noticed when she walked in the doctor's office was that another door besides the twins' was closed. That meant another patient.

From the desk, Lexi looked up. She brightened. "Why, hello, Amethyst! How nice to see you again! The twins have been practically *begging* for you! They'll be so delighted!"

Dr. Sawyer exited out of the closed door. He seemed surprised to see them. "Amethyst!"

"Dr. Sawyer. Nice you see you again," said Amethyst. "We came by to see if the twins were cured yet."

"Are they," said the doctor. "And there's somebody else here who wants to see you, too. Lexi, would you get our patient out of her room?" Lexi nodded obediently and went into the other room. She closed the door behind her.

Amethyst's heart started to beat. *Was there any chance - any chance at all - at all - that it was Miranda?*

Dr. Sawyer saw her surprise. "You must be surprised. She was wandering around a field when Lexi found her while driving to KFC to pick up our dinner. She was very weak for a bit, but she's practically cured now." He went, upset, to the door and peaked in. "Lexi, our guests are waiting."

Amethyst heard Lexi sigh. She whispered to Josh, "Do you.... do you.... think there's any chance.... it's Miranda?"

Josh frowned. "Well, if our magic worked, she *did* end up in a prairie, or field, but there's millions of girls in America, Amethyst, and-"

Amethyst cut him off. "But she *wants to see me*, Josh. Seriously, I'm *not* a celebrity! A regular girl off the street wouldn't want to see me!" Her heart was beating even more rapidly now, because what Josh said was true. She came from a field, and that's where Miranda would be.

Lexi came out of the room, and Miranda was with her.

Amethyst's heart filled with joy. She rushed forward and hugged Miranda until the girl said, "You're suffocating me!"

Amethyst let her go. Miranda studied her. "You found me."

Amethyst nodded and gave her another quick hug. "You don't know what we've been through to get you."

Miranda gave her a look. "I probably do. But what I want to know is, what happened between the time you were put on the orphan train to now to get you here? And who are these other people?" She gestured to the group.

McKenna stormed to the front. "Listen, you might be-"

Courtney sighed. "Stop it, McKenna." She extended her hand. "Hi. I'm Courtney, and that's McKenna."

McKenna frowned and shot Miranda a sour look.

Oh boy, this could get bad, Amethyst thought, but even so she grinned. Their quest was complete! Finally, once they destroyed the evil fairies and found a safe place for the ring, the world would be a peaceful place again!

After introductions, Miranda repeated, "How did you get here?" and Amethyst had to tell the whole story, from being thrown in the boxcar to finding Mary to discovering the ring to tracking Miranda herself down.

At the end Miranda stood, gaping. "No way," she breathed.

"The boxcar - the boxcar - I was - I was on it," she stammered in excitement, "and I - I still have friends living on it!" Her voice became desperate.

As someone who had also made friends and been separated for a time being, Amethyst completely understood. "Sister, you don't worry about that one little bit. I had friends in that situation, too."

"But you didn't get them back," said Miranda sadly, "so there's little chance I'll get mine back."

Amethyst was stunned, and she began laughing. "Miranda, that's just it! I *did* get my friends back!" She gestured to the group. Suddenly from the outside, Mary came in. She had been waiting outside for some strange reason that she wouldn't tell Amethyst. She saw Miranda and rushed over, giving her a hug even though they had never met. Miranda stood stiffly until Mary stopped hugging her.

Then Mary's gaze drifted to Dr. Sawyer. They began to talk.

Amethyst found this funny but decided to shrug it off. She turned to Miranda. "Sister, I did get my friends back. So we'll get yours back, too!"

"Okay -" Miranda did a double take. "Wait, did you call me *sister?*"

Amethyst nodded. "How's it going?" she said. "I thought you'd know for some weird reason. We're sisters! Twin sisters! And guess what! Emmy and Rachel are our little twin sisters! Mary knows my- I mean, our- mother and she told me!" Miranda's eyes glittered.

"Suddenly I love the twins!" she cried.

As if on cue, the twins rushed out of their room. "Big sissy!" they screamed, hugging Amethyst. Amethyst laughed. "You mean big *sissies!*" she told them. "Miranda's your big sissy too!"

"Yippee!" cried the twins, hugging Miranda.

Mary was over by Lexi. She looked up at Amethyst, smiling slyly. "I bet Emmy and Rachel'll love having three big sisters." Amethyst frowned. "You counted wrong, Mary, there's only two of us."

Mary placed her hands on Lexi's shoulders. "Meet your

biggest sister, Opal."

Amethyst heard Mary's words. She heard them. But her brain didn't register them. It was like Mary's words seemed so impossible, her brain just blocked it out as a possibility. *It must be April Fools' Day*, Amethyst thought, even though she knew it wasn't true. Out loud, she said, "Excuse me, I didn't quite catch that."

Mary closed her eyes and repeated, "Lexi's real name is Opal. She's your sister."

It took a few minutes for the words to sink in.

"You're.... you're.... tricking me," said Amethyst. Lexi - or Opal - couldn't be her sister, because Dr. Sawyer was her father, but not Amethyst's! "Lexi... Opal.... has a father, I don't."

Mary kept her eyes closed, not saying anything.

Lexi said, "I..... it's true, Amethyst."

Amethyst blinked. "Why didn't you tell me earlier," she said without any questioning in her voice.

"I didn't know earlier."

Dr. Sawyer put a hand on Lexi's shoulder.

"Mary?" he asked, obviously leaving something out.

Mary nodded.

Amethyst took Miranda's hand. "Do you have any idea what is going on?"

"Not any more than you do," responded Miranda, sounding just as curious. "Whatever news Dr. Sawyer gives you will be just as surprising to me because we're in the same family now." Her eyes glistened. She was very excited.

Amethyst looked down at the twins. Rachel was by her side, and Emmy by Miranda's. They had not listened to Mary at all and were simply giggling and saying over and over, "We have big sissies, we have big sissies!" in a quiet whisper.

Dr. Sawyer said, "I am Lexi's father. Lexi is your sister. Does that connect anything?"

It did, but Amethyst's mouth was so dry she couldn't say anything. *Maybe she wasn't an orphan after all. If Dr. Sawyer is right, then he's my....* She felt pride in thinking it - *he's my father. But do I have a mother, and if I do, where is she?*

Dr. Sawyer smiled, but before he spoke, Mary said, "We'll explain everything later."

Courtney spoke up. "If you didn't know earlier how do you know now? And do you know if I have any parents, or siblings?"

"I know," said Mary. "I'll tell you later." She looked nervous. "*After* we rescue Miranda's friends. What train were you on, Miranda honey cake?"

Miranda shrugged. "The same one Amethyst traveled on, I believe."

Mary turned to Amethyst.

"Uh, I was on boxcar twenty-four?" said Amethyst.

"What a lot of help that does," said Mary. "Okay, we'll just go to the nearest station. Lexi, Dr. Sawyer, care to come along?"

Dr. Sawyer shook his head at the same time Lexi nodded.

That reminded Amethyst of a peculiar person she had met. Avery. Where was Avery now? Was she good? Was she bad? Was she on their side, or not? What about Steve and Andrew? Would they have to defeat Jenny and Mrs. Mia?

Mary laughed. "Do you mind if we take Lexi along?" Dr. Sawyer was worried. "Okay, I guess.... but keep her safe for me."

Mary laughed. "You know I will." After bidding goodbye, she led the now party of people outside and sat them down.

Amethyst said, "I wonder what happened to Avery."

"Avery?" Mary was puzzled. Amethyst repeated the whole story about the Mochas. When they were done Mary nodded. "After we rescue the friends, let's track her down. We need to know what side she's on as soon as possible."

Amethyst nodded, although she didn't see the importance. With Mary in the lead and Lexi in the back, they went down narrow streets and through the city of Donut until they found the train station.

Mary walked into the station and found a newsletter labeled "Orphan Train" and picked it up, the same thing she had done what seemed like an eternity ago when they were looking for Amethyst's friends. It had been almost a year since Amethyst's tenth birthday.

Almost a year.... almost a year.... That meant Amethyst's

eleventh birthday was coming soon! What month was it? - Amethyst's birthday was February 24. "What month is it? What day?" Amethyst begged.

"February 23, I believe," murmured Mary, leafing through the newsletter. "Why would you like to know? I admit, it is quite warm for February."

Amethyst looked at Miranda. "Our birthday's tomorrow," she cheered.

Miranda smiled largely.

"Eleven," said Mary dreamily. "Eleven." Then she went back to the newsletter. "We're in luck. The orphan train is supposed to arrive any minute." She went back out front and cocked her head to one side. "In fact, I hear it already."

chapter thirty-nine
Back to
Boxcar 24

Everyone rushed to Mary's side to listen. Indeed, it was coming. The shrill, off-key whistle could be heard from miles away. And even so, at miles off, it made Amethyst cover her ears in disgust. Mary even looked disgusted.

"Mary? I thought orphan trains arrived at asylums," said Amethyst, puzzled.

"It does," said Mary. "It'll speed right past us, on its way."

Amethyst nodded. "So we need to get to the asylum first. Come, let's go!"

But Mary shook her head. "No, honey cake. We'll stop it here."

"How?" Emily wanted to know.

"By waving. Pretend you're mistaking the orphan train for a passenger train ·"

"Mary. The orphan train has huge letters declaring its name on its side."

"Well then, pretend you can't read."

They agreed. Soon Amethyst leaned out and saw a dim light coming. "It's coming!" she cried.

Mary leaned out and saw it, too. "Positions, everyone, and be ready to wave and shout," said Mary briskly. "The train'll stop, because that's what any kind train would do."

A few minutes later, Amethyst was impatient. She leaned out again. The train was slowing down. Perhaps it *did* stop here? But that wouldn't make any sense, unless the orphan-train rules had changed and orphans were picked up at train stations. But there were no poor children anywhere in sight.

As the train began to roll past, Amethyst started waving emphatically. With an almost annoyed screech of the brakes, the train came to a halt. An annoyed conductor leaned out.

"Whaddaya want?" he said through his teeth.

Amethyst had no idea what they wanted. Mary had never said what to say. Luckily, Mary herself spoke up. "When does the orphan train come through here, sir?"

"This *is* the orphan train," growled the conductor. "What's wrong with ya, lady? Can't you read a simple few words?"

Mary ignored him. "Oh, so this is the orphan train! Come along, kids." She leaned forward on the door, and with a click, it opened.

The conductor was startled. "Hey, whaddaya doin'?" he cried.

"These poor kids have always wanted to see the inside of an orphan train," Mary said, her voice dripping with pity. "So I told them, 'Darlings, whenever that orphan train a-rolls through here, we'll a-stop it and board it."

"But this isn't a passenger train!" yelled the conductor. "It's an orphan train!"

I can pay whatever you ask," said Mary, gesturing for them to sit. She pulled out some money from her pocket. "What do you want? Ten, twenty?"

The conductor looked interested. "It'll cost fifty."

Mary blew on the money and then gave him a fifty-dollar bill.

He inspected it, as if he thought it might blow up, and then nodded. After the door closed with a creak, the train started up again.

Once the conductor had gone back to driving in the little compartment at the front of the train, Mary sighed loudly. "This air is so thick and damp!" she complained. Then she rolled her eyes. "Miranda? What boxcar was it?"

Miranda looked puzzled. "What -"

"The one you were on," finished Mary.

"Oh. Boxcar twenty... four?" said Miranda. "I'm pretty sure."

Before it was open all the way, Miranda stopped her. "There was someone named Nora -"

Mary nodded. "She's not here, at least not at this moment. Come, let's hurry." The group filed into the next car, then the next. Finally, Miranda touched Mary's arm. "This next car is it."

* * * * * * * * * * * * * * * * * * *

Delaney knew she heard noises outside the boxcar. And she knew it had to be Miranda. But she didn't bother telling anybody, because she knew they wouldn't believe her. They'd just have to wait and see.

The noises became louder. Delaney wanted to squirm. Could Miranda just open up already?

* * * * * * * * * * * * * * * * * * *

Mary looked from the door to Miranda. "Would you like to?" Miranda nodded. She took a deep breath and placed her hand on the door handle. She grabbed the door handle and pulled it slowly.

"Just what do you think you're doing?"

chapter forty
Marshibilsn!

Heads swung, all but Miranda's. Her eyes were fixed on the doorhandle. It was almost all the way pulled.... almost....

Amethyst stared at Nora. She was wearing a blue hat embedded with jewels, but no hair peeked out from underneath, obviously because she had no hair left. Amethyst almost giggled.

"What do you think you are doing?" repeated Nora. "Why are you in my boxcar, why are you in my train, why are you anywhere?"

Amethyst snapped her fingers, but nothing emerged.

Nora laughed, a wicked, evil laugh. "Magic doesn't work on good fairies in here," she said in a teasing tone.

Miranda swung the door open.

Nora noticed. "MARSHIBILSN!" she shouted in fury, and then two things happened at once.

First of all, "marshibilsn" was also the key word to unfreeze, so Delaney, Rebecca, and Kayla were unfrozen. The second thing was, when Nora was so obsessed with yelling, she had been backing up, and she hadn't seen the open door leading to the next car in her way. She stumbled and tripped out of the boxcar, her screams echoing across the whole land.

Miranda swung the door open, and Delaney, Rebecca, and Kayla rushed out, hugging her emphatically and saying how-are-yous and what-happened-to-yous and I'm-so-glad-to-see-yous. Finally, Delaney noticed the group of people behind Miranda, all staring in confusion at them.

Kayla spotted Courtney in the group, and her eyes widened.

She rushed over to Courtney in excitement. "Court!" she exclaimed. "Is it really you?"

Courtney smacked a hand to her mouth. "Kayla?"

Kayla gave her a watery grin. "I knew I'd find you someday, Miss Court." She smiled again.

Aghast, Miranda said, "How do you know her?" to Kayla at the exact time Amethyst said it to *Courtney.*

Kayla said, "Remember what I told you in the boxcar, Miranda? We came from the same asylum."

Courtney said teasingly, "Have you brushed your hair Kay?"

Kayla giggled.

Delaney walked up to McKenna and stuck out her hand. "Sup, I'm Delaney, it's nice to meet you," she said.

"Uh, hi," said McKenna. "I'm McKenna. Who are you?"

"I told you, I'm Delaney," sang Delaney. "I'm Miranda's friend, and I will be till the end."

"I see," said McKenna. "Well, I'm Amethyst's friend, and I'll be hers till the end." She stopped, looked at Courtney, and whispered, "But I'm not friends with Courtney, and I might be friends with her till the end."

Delaney looked puzzled. "Who's Amethyst? Who's Courtney?" and so Mary introduced everyone. After that, Mary led everyone out.

"Okay, now I'm *really* embarrassed," said Josh, looking around at the girls surrounding him. "There's like five million girls surrounding me, and I'm a boy."

Amethyst laughed. "Don't be embarrassed, Josh."

Josh scoffed, but he wasn't mad. "Easy for you to say. You're a *girl* surrounded by *girls!*" He acted mad, but Amethyst knew he wasn't.

Mary silenced the pack. "Let's all head back to my house. I have a few things to tell y'all."

Amethyst nodded. Mary led the way back to the conductor and ended up paying him more to make a special stop for them. They got off, and after they had regrouped, Mary turned to Amethyst and asked her to use the Ring to bring them to her house, along with Dr. Sawyer. Amethyst began to say *No, let's walk!* but then she sighed and resented, and then wished it.

Amethyst expected the weird feelings again, but this time, she felt comfort. Instead of roughly spinning, she was gently spinning. Her eyes didn't sting, her legs didn't bend wrong ways. She felt peace.

Amethyst suddenly remembered a question she wanted to ask Mary. *I'll ask her when we get there,* she decided.
Amethyst shut her eyes, and when she opened them, they were in Mary's house, in the front room. Dr. Sawyer was there. "I'm glad you wished him here, Amethyst. I wanted him to be part of this telling."

Amethyst wondered what the telling could be. What would Mary need to tell her? She already knew the twins, Miranda, and Lexi were her sisters. What else did she need to know?

That reminded her. "Mary, can I ask a question?"

"Sure," said Mary. "We have time."

"Well...." Amethyst said, "when we were using our sparking abilities to fight Nora and the crew, why didn't you let me use the ring then?"

Mary said, "Because I don't want you to rely only on the ring for safety. You need to know you have powers, too."

Amethyst frowned. Powers? Oh, yeah, the sparks.

Mary asked, "Is that all?"

"What? Oh, yes," said Amethyst. "I'm done."

chapter forty-one
Fairies!

Mary started, taking a deep breath. "Miranda..... Amethyst.... Emmy.... Rachel.... Lexi.... you're not orphans."

"I know," said Lexi. "Dad - he's Dr. Sawyer -"

"Yes, but where's your mother?"

Lexi had no answer.

Amethyst was excited. "Mary.... where's my mom?" She did a double take. "Wait....." Yes, that was right. "Dr. Sawyer's my dad, but -"

Mary looked at Dr. Sawyer. "Care to tell them?"

"Of course." Dr. Sawyer stood up. "Mary - she's your mother."

Mary is my mother? Amethyst didn't believe it. She couldn't believe it. But yet— she did believe it. She knew it was true. It was unbelievable. All she could think was: *Mary is my mother, Mary is my mother, Mary is my mother, my mother.*

Her mother. Who she had longed for all those years at the asylum.

Amethyst began to smile. But she had a question. "Why didn't you tell me earlier?"

"I was waiting for the perfect time," said Mary. "Besides, I didn't want you getting distracted from your quest."

Amethyst smiled, looking at her newfound parents. "All this time....." Then she grinned, ran forward, and wrapped her arms around Mary, then Dr. Sawyer. Miranda was quick to follow, along with the twins (who didn't really understand, of course, but did it because everyone else was).

Mary took another deep breath, once the hugging was done. "I have another surprising fact to tell you. You know on the train, where Eugenia made you snap your fingers and such? Well you can do that because you're all part-fairies." She loosened her sweater, revealing a beautiful pair of fairy wings. "I'm a fairy, Dr. Sawyer's not. For the rest of you guys...." She looked out at the rest of the group.

"Yes?" asked McKenna.

"You guys are descendants from fairies as well. I haven't been able to find those relatives yet, however, but in a moment I'll tell you who's sisters and brothers with who."

"Okay," they said.

Amethyst blinked, realizing exactly what Mary had said. "No. That's not possible for us to be fairies." But still, she knew it had to be true.

"Wait," said Emily. "It is. Why else would just us be put in boxcars, be the ones the evil fairies want to capture? It makes perfect sense!"

Amethyst's eyes widened in realization. "And.... at the asylum when I was being boarded Miss Odelia or somebody was running late with getting the orphans together and they were all frazzled and Miss Odelia was like 'we don't have all the orphans' and Mrs. Vancolia was like 'are any of them....'! She must've meant 'are any of them fairies?'!"

Mary smiled, nodding to say Amethyst was correct. "Lucy...... your mother was the fairy queen, but since she was.... gotten rid of, you are now."

Lucy grinned, snuggling her doll, Marissa. "That's awesome."

Mary said, "Since I will be caring for lots of girls -" She looked at Josh - "and one boy, I need a few people to volunteer to help Lucy at the castle her mother left for her."

"I'll do it," said Delaney.

"So will I," said Kayla. "I barely know anybody here, anyhow."

Rebecca hesitated. "I want to be with Miranda, but -"

"It's fine," Miranda told her. "Besides, we'll visit a lot."

"I'll go," said Angelica.

"Mom?" said Amethyst. "I have a question. How - why - how did I get to the asylum in the first place? And where did I live before?"

Mary sighed and closed her eyes. "Well.... let me start from the beginning."

Everyone scooted closer.

"You see, the evil fairies like Mahalia and Eugenia were against me very much. When Opal, or Lexi, was born, Dr Sawyer and I were very worried the evil fairies would find out about her, so we kept it very secret, until she was about six or seven. Nothing had happened yet so we decided to have another child." She smiled at Miranda and Amethyst. "But it turned out to be non-identical twins." She took a deep breath. "We were overjoyed. But the day after you were born, Mahalia found out and she stole you from me in the middle of the night, and took you to the asylum. Dr. Sawyer and I ... we were just devastated. Not a day passed where we didn't search. We looked for seven years, then I got pregnant with the twins. But when they were two days old Mahalia stole them from me. Then Sawyer and I knew that Opal, or Lexi, was in danger now. So he took her and went to work as a doctor, to raise Lexi as a normal human child."

Amethyst had a question. "Why - why wasn't Miranda called..."

Mary closed her eyes. "Sawyer.... is it time...."

The doctor nodded faintly.

"Well," said Mary, "you all have jeweled fairy names. And jeweled fairy names have power."

"Power?"

"You can do amazing things, girls," said Mary. "My kids, at least. When we arrived at the asylum, Odelia was aware of that. So she began to call Miranda Miranda, and since Miranda was so young she adapted to it. The same thing happened with the twins." She looked curiously at Amethyst.

Amethyst smiled. "I know mine. Until I was four, Mary, they called me Ellie. But when I was four, one of my teachers accidentally called me Amethyst. I asked her why she called me that and she said it was my true name." Amethyst felt very proud telling the story. "I was mad when I learned I wasn't being called my given name. I demanded everyone call me Amethyst."

Mary laughed. "Good job, honey cake."

"So... I have powers?" asked Emmy. When Mary nodded, she jumped up and spun with Rachel in a circle. "We're powerful girls," they sang.

Mary stopped them. "The only way you have power is if you're called by your true name." She paused. "Now.... siblings."

Everyone grinned.

"First off...Emily, you and Josh are sibs."

Josh let out a groan, but he really was kind of excited to have a sister. Emily smiled, happy to have a brother.

"Angelica, you're sisters with, believe it or not, Kayla."

"What!" cried Kayla, then, "Cool." She looked at Angelica awkwardly. Angelica grinned back.

"The rest of you are only children, except for Courtney and McKenna......" She took a deep breath. "Uh..... you guys are sisters."

McKenna sat down and put her head in her hands in fake anger. Everyone laughed.

"I'm not sure where all your parents are," said Mary. "But I'm trying my best to locate them."

And right then, Amethyst knew. She knew why the name *honey cake* had sounded so familiar. That's what her mother - rather, Mary - had called her before she was stolen.

Mary smiled, seeing Amethyst's realization, sitting on the couch by Dr. Sawyer.

And when nobody was looking, Amethyst slipped her hand into her pocket, pulled out the Ring, and glanced at it, and grinned wider than ever.

For the ring had not taken shape of a sapphire, garnet, or diamond. Not even a topaz or peridot.

It was an amethyst.

EPILOGUE

Delaney, Rebecca, Kayla, and Angelica went to help Lucy in her ruling, and she was a fine ruler. The ring was put in the Fairy museum, where it was safe. (Plans are being made to return it to its home beneath the sea.) Mary and Dr. Sawyer took care of Amethyst and her sisters, along with McKenna, Courtney, Josh, and Emily. Josh never stopped being embarrassed about being the only boy.

After a while, they did go back and take over Mahalia's castle. All her servants were sick of being mean, so they were happy to go help Lucy instead.

As for Avery and Steve... well, after a few weeks, Mary went to find them. Steve was happy to leave his evil mother, Jenny, and help Lucy. Avery couldn't decide if she should be nice or evil, so she stayed living with her mom. Andrew went to live with Steve at Lucy's castle also, which made Jenny infuriated.

Amethyst and Miranda (rather, Emerald) had a very happy eleventh birthday. They received many presents (including a pretend form of the ring from Mary). They had a party at Lucy's castle and Amethyst and Miranda got to eat birthday cake for the first time in their lives. And gradually the five adapted to being called their given names.

ABOUT THE AUTHOR

J.C. Buchanan is 12 years old and has been writing stories and books since she was four. When she is not writing, she enjoys reading, drawing, and hanging with her awesome friends. This is her first novel ever. She lives in Illinois with her mom, dad, and her three younger brothers.

To find out more about *The Hidden Amethyst* or to contact J.C., check out her blog; she'd love to hear from you!

thehiddenamethyst.blogspot.com

54656947R00107

Made in the USA
Charleston, SC
11 April 2016